Ple
on

To
or

You

YOUNG HEROES

For my niece and nephews, the most amazing children I know!
-LB

To all the children who will read it. I hope this book can
encourage them to pursue their dreams! With commitment
and dedication anyone can achieve their desired success
-FF

To all the little ones, who make me believe
that everything is possible
-IM

To Olivia and Ryan
-JS

STRIPES PUBLISHING
An imprint of the Little Tiger Group
1 Coda Studios, 189 Munster Road, London SW6 6AW

First published in Great Britain in 2018

Text copyright © Lula Bridgeport, 2018
Illustrations copyright © Federica Frenna, Isabel Muñoz and Julianna Swaney, 2018

ISBN: 978-1-84715-955-7

A CIP catalogue record for this book is available from the British Library.

Printed and bound in China.

2 4 6 8 10 9 7 5 3 1

YOUNG HEROES

Written by Lula Bridgeport

Illustrated by
Federica Frenna, Isabel Muñoz
and Julianna Swaney

Stripes

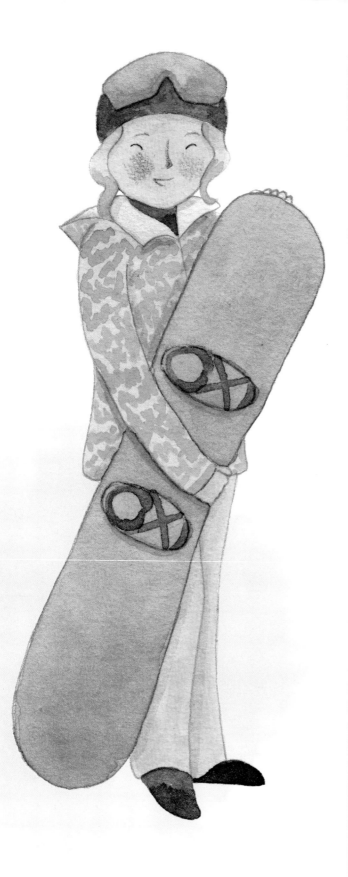

Chloe Kim

Snowboarder – see page 89.

Contents

INTRODUCTION

Do you ever wonder what it would be like to change the world? Are you passionate about a particular hobby or cause, or always coming up with new ideas? Do you dream of making your community a better, happier and safer place for all?

Sometimes it only takes one person to make a change. And what's even more exciting is that you don't have to wait until you're older to do it – you can be amazing at any age! From impressive inventors to awesome artists, this book is a celebration of the children, teenagers and young adults who dreamed big, aimed high and have already made an awesome contribution to the world.

First up we have the children from STEM: young scientists, tech wizards, engineers and mathematicians, whose inventions and discoveries are changing and saving lives.

Then there are the stars of Film and Music, talented actors and musicians who dazzle audiences around the world.

Where would we be without the children who devote their lives to saving the Environment for future generations? How about the child champions and record-breakers of Sport, who encourage us to strive to be our best every day?

Life would be so very dull without the young entrepreneurs and inventors of the Business world, or the talented artists, writers and dancers of the Arts and Literature world. Finally, we celebrate the children who dedicate their lives to making the world a better place through Politics and Activism.

Each of the children in this book has something in common – they are not afraid to stand out, speak up and work hard to achieve their goals. Maybe their incredible stories will inspire you to follow in their footsteps?

Childhood Through Time

You may think it's hard being a kid today, but spare a thought for the children of the past – life could be so tough in ancient cultures that many children didn't even make it past childhood! If a child did survive, they had very few of the freedoms that most young people enjoy today. Boys were usually favoured over girls, while almost all children had to work for a living instead of going to school. In fact, life only started to get better for children in the late nineteenth and early twentieth centuries, when governments began to pass laws that protected their rights and freedoms.

3300BC–1700BC

Indus Valley Civilization
Pakistan and Northwest India

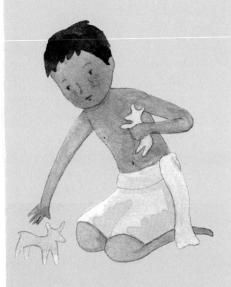

It was so hot in the Indus Valley that children played outside in the courtyards and streets, and on the flat roofs of their homes to keep cool. Sometimes they'd even sleep on the roof at night!

3100BC–332BC

Ancient Egyptians
Northeast Africa

One in every two or three Ancient Egyptian babies died from disease before the age of one. Mothers tied amulets (small pieces of jewellery) to their newborns to ward off "evil spirits", and carried their babies in slings to protect them from scorpions and snakes.

1000BC–AD1521

Ancient Mayans
Mexico and Central America

Ancient Mayan parents bound babies' heads between two wooden boards for several years to give them a flat, sloping forehead. They also dangled objects in front of their baby's face until the baby's eyes were permanently crossed!

753BC–AD476

Ancient Romans
Mediterranean and
Western Europe

Ancient Roman girls were married
from twelve. The night before her
wedding day, a girl removed her
lunula (birth charm) and returned
it to her parents. She also gave
away all her toys, as a symbol of
her childhood coming to an end.

AD793–1066

Vikings
Denmark, Norway and
Sweden (Scandinavia)

Viking fathers trained their sons as
warriors from an early age. They
taught them to fight with swords,
spears and axes. Stronger girls were
also allowed to train as warriors.
Boys learned how to build and
repair boats, and were taught to
navigate oceans using landmarks
and the stars in the night sky.

AD500–1500

Middle Ages
Europe

During the Middle Ages, houses
were often dirty, dark and cold,
so mothers swaddled their babies
in cloth to keep them warm and
snug. At night, older siblings
huddled together on a hay
mattress on the floor.

AD900–1897

Kingdom of Benin
Southern Nigeria

In the Kingdom of Benin, there were no schools. Children learned from parents and elders. Boys were responsible for sweeping and clearing the forest paths that surrounded their village. Girls were expected to collect firewood and water, and carry pottery and textiles to market.

1195–1522

Aztecs
Central Mexico

Aztec parents loved their children but they gave strict punishments. One was to hold the naughty child over a chilli-pepper fire until the smoke stung and burned the child's eyes, nose and mouth.

1271–1911

Late Imperial China
China

During the Late Imperial period in China, all but the poorest girls had their feet bound from the age of six, as small feet were seen as beautiful. First the girl's feet were soaked in a mixture of herbs and hot water. Then her toes were broken and curled underneath her feet before being bound with strips of cotton or silk. The girls wore tiny shoes to hold the bandages in place.

1485–1603

Tudors
England

1760–1901

The Industrial Revolution
and the Victorians
Great Britain

1914–1918

The First World War
Europe

Water was so dirty during Tudor times that everyone – including children – drank weak beer or ale! It may seem strange today, but beer was actually safer to drink because the brewing process killed many of the nasty germs in the water.

Girls and boys as young as four worked for more than twelve hours a day in factories, textile mills and coalmines, or as chimney sweeps or servants for rich families. Many died or were injured as a result. Child workers were also beaten with a leather strap or stick for talking, singing or leaving their place of work without permission.

During the First World War, around a quarter of a million British boys, many as young as fourteen, lied about their age in order to join the army. The same happened in Germany. Over 30,000 teenage soldiers on both sides were killed or wounded during the Battle of the Somme (July–November 1916).

STEM

Do you ever wonder how machines work? Perhaps you have a talent for maths or love coming up with new inventions? Maybe you're fascinated by technology, and dream of making your very own video game or launching a rocket to Mars? If any of the above sounds like you, then you are a fan of STEM!

STEM stands for Science, Technology, Engineering and Mathematics. It attracts many of the world's most gifted and curious minds. Why? Because not only is STEM fun but it can also transform lives. Through science and mathematics we are able to understand and engage with the world around us, from curing disease and protecting the environment to solving the mysteries of the universe. Technology is rapidly changing the way we live, while we rely on engineering to make buildings, vehicles and machines work.

The people involved in STEM are true pioneers – they not only solve many of the problems facing society today but they're also building a brighter future. And what better group to reimagine that future than children? Take Kelvin Doe, Ann Makosinski and Richard Turere, whose engineering inventions are already changing lives. If you want to know about children saving lives, look no further than budding research scientists Sarah Sobka and Krtin Nithiyanandam, whose medical discoveries have given hope to millions suffering with disease. George Matus and Marita Cheng have turned their passion for drones and robots into successful businesses, while Nick D'Aloisio and Jacob Barnett are using their knowledge to solve some of life's biggest problems.

These young innovators, inventors and entrepreneurs are already making a difference. Perhaps their amazing stories will inspire you to join them?

George Matus

1998– | DRONE ENGINEER | USA

When eleven-year-old George Matus and his family moved to Salt Lake City in Utah, USA, he found himself living in an enormous natural playground. Salt Lake City is surrounded by snow-capped mountains, and what better way to explore them than from way up in the sky? George bought a remote control (RC) helicopter and attached a camera to it. When he uploaded the footage to YouTube, the helicopter's makers saw it and invited him to become a test pilot. The schoolboy had soon tested every RC aircraft, and drones became his passion.

But what exactly is a drone? Think of it as a tiny aircraft but without a pilot on board. Instead, it is operated from the ground by remote control. Not only are drones fun to fly but they're also a safer alternative to sending a person into a dangerous area, such as a battlefield or disaster zone.

George spent every spare moment flying and adapting drones but he soon grew frustrated. Most drones are designed for one job: some are built for racing, others to capture footage of the Earth from the clouds. Why couldn't a single drone do all these things? That's when George began creating his "wish list" for the perfect drone.

At sixteen, George won a grant from the Thiel Foundation, which invests in young entrepreneurs, to develop his drone. Several years later, he'd built Teal and Teal 2, the world's fastest battery-operated drones. Teal 1 and 2 can reach speeds of up to 137kmh (85mph). Best of all, they do every job on George's wish list.

Today, George is flying high. At eighteen, he became founder and chief executive of Teal Drones, while his dream drones are now being sold around the world. You could say that his idea really took off!

"Really find what interests you, and then it doesn't feel like work."

Sarah Sobka

1998– | RESEARCH SCIENTIST | UK

In 2015, seventeen-year-old Sarah Sobka was named the UK's Young Scientist of the Year. Sarah had been volunteering for a University of Sheffield team that was testing the effects of the drug lubiprostone on cystic fibrosis (CF). CF is a genetic disease (meaning a person is born with it). The disease affects around 100,000 people across the world. People with CF lack the gene that controls the movement of salt and water in and out of the cells of their body. This causes their lungs and other organs to fill with thick, sticky mucus, making it hard for them to breathe and digest food.

Current CF drugs are expensive and don't always work. Lubiprostone is a cheaper drug used to treat women with another disease, irritable bowel syndrome. Now a full-time medical student, Sarah is hopeful that her initial research will go on to help find a cheaper, more effective cure that could one day save thousands of lives.

Kelvin Doe

1996– | ENGINEER | SIERRA LEONE

Kelvin Doe has a curious mind and endless imagination. Growing up poor in Freetown, Sierra Leone, Kelvin taught himself to build radios, transmitters and generators from scrap metal he found in the city's rubbish dumps. By sixteen, he had built his own radio station and was broadcasting across Freetown as DJ Focus.

After reaching the finals of Global Minimum Inc's competition for young African inventors, Kelvin was invited to the USA to attend a programme at the Massachusetts Institute of Technology (MIT), making him the university's youngest-ever "visiting practitioner". Then, a YouTube documentary about Kelvin went viral, with 12.3 million views to date! Kelvin's life changed overnight, and in 2012 he flew to the USA to share his inspirational story on the TEDxTeen stage.

Today, Kelvin runs his own company, KDoe-Tech Inc, through which he teaches young people that they too can create something from nothing. All it takes is creativity, passion and belief.

Richard Turere

1998– | INVENTOR OF LION LIGHTS | KENYA

Nairobi National Park in southwest Kenya is known as the "Wildlife Capital of the World". Each year millions of tourists flock to the park to see elephants, rhinos and big cats roam freely here. But the park is no wilderness: just 7km (4miles) separates these wild plains from Kenya's capital city, Nairobi, and the 6.5 million people living there. And when herd animals migrate, their predators follow…

Richard Turere grew up disliking lions. As a member of the Maasai tribe, he lived on a farm on the national park's borders. Like many boys his age, it was nine-year-old Richard's job to herd his father's cattle and protect them from the predators that wandered on to the farm, looking for an easy meal. It could be a grim job: some mornings he would wake up to discover that lions had attacked in the night, killing valuable livestock. He wasn't the only one. Livestock loss is a common problem in Kenya. Some farmers would poison entire prides in order to protect their cattle, damaging the park's lion population – and its tourist figures – in the process.

The young Maasai boy believed there had to be a better way, so he put his imagination to the test. His first idea was to use fire. But rather than scaring the lions, the orange flames only drew them closer to the farm. Next, knowing that lions are frightened of humans, Richard built a life-like scarecrow. But these were clever cats. They soon learned that the scarecrow was a trick, since it never moved. Finally, Richard was patrolling the farm with a torch at dusk when he had another bright idea: wild

animals associate the flickering torchlight with humans. That night, the lions stayed away.

Richard leaped into action. In his spare time, he enjoyed pulling apart and rebuilding radios. He figured he could use his knowledge of electronics to build his new invention: "Lion Lights". Gathering a car battery, an indicator box (which makes vehicle indicators "blink"), a solar panel and a light bulb, Richard rigged up an electrical circuit around the farm. It worked: the flashing lights fooled the lions into believing that Richard was patrolling the farm with a torch, when he was actually asleep in his bed!

The hungry lions never returned. When other farmers saw the results, they asked Richard to install the lights on their fences. Since then, Lion Lights have been used on farms across Kenya and they're helping to keep other large predators, such as leopards and hyenas, at bay.

Richard's brilliant invention soon caught the attention of local conservationist Paula Kahumbu. She helped Richard to win a scholarship to one of Kenya's best schools, putting him one step closer to fulfilling his dream of becoming an engineer and pilot. In 2013, he was also invited to the USA to tell his story on the TED stage. Now, thanks to Richard, lion numbers in Naoribi National Park are growing again while farmers – and their cattle – can finally sleep easy.

"One year ago I was just a boy herding my father's cows. Now I want to be an engineer and pilot."

Ann Makosinski

1997– | INVENTOR | CANADA

When Ann Makosinski learned that a friend in the Philippines was struggling to study at night because her family couldn't afford electricity, she knew she had to help. Ann had an idea for a torch that could run without batteries or electricity. She began experimenting with cheap materials, including electrical circuits and a special generator that converts heat into power. She soon discovered that the materials could produce enough energy to run a light bulb simply through body heat: as soon as someone picks up the torch, it starts to shine.

The Hollow Flashlight was a dazzling success. In 2013, Ann won first place in the Google Science Fair's 15–16 age category. The following year, at just seventeen, she appeared in *Time* magazine's 30 Under 30 list. Now a student at the University of British Columbia, Canada, Ann hopes that her "light bulb moment" will brighten people's lives around the world.

Nick D'Aloisio

1995– | COMPUTER PROGRAMMER | UK

British schoolboy Nick D'Aloisio was just eleven years old when an app he invented in his bedroom caught Apple's interest. "Trimit" condensed long news articles into short summaries, making it possible for smartphone users to read the articles on the go. After winning over £1 million in investment, Nick redesigned the app as "Summly" in 2011.
It was a smash hit, with over 200,000 downloads! Nick also won several major tech awards and was featured in *Business Insider* and *Wired* magazines.

But the best was yet to come: in 2013, Summly was sold to Yahoo for around $30 million, making the seventeen-year-old one of the world's youngest self-made millionaires. However, Nick hasn't let the success go to his head. While working on his new company, Sphere, he is studying for a degree at Oxford University – in computer science, of course!

Krtin Nithiyanandam

2000– | RESEARCH SCIENTIST | UK

When Krtin Nithiyanandam had surgery on his ear as a child, rather than put him off hospitals for life, it sparked his fascination with medical science. But it was an article about Alzheimer's disease that spurred the schoolboy into action. The brain disease, and others like it, causes memory loss and confusion, making it difficult to speak, think and solve problems. These diseases affect around 44 million people across the world. They are also difficult to spot in the early stages, which can lead to problems with treatment. But Krtin was sure he could find a solution.

He learned that certain types of toxic proteins appear in the brain in the first stages of Alzheimer's. Finding them could be the key to an early diagnosis … but how would doctors get to them? Cue Krtin! The fifteen-year-old began by testing different antibodies and their reaction to Alzheimer's proteins. Antibodies are a part of the body's defence system. They detect cells that cause disease and set off a warning system for other, healthy cells to attack them. But for this to work for Alzheimer's, Krtin needed to figure out a way to get the antibodies into the brain.

With the help of scientists at Surrey University, Krtin created an antibody solution that doctors could inject directly into the brain. Once there, the antibodies would "latch on" to the Alzheimer's proteins. Adding a coloured dye to the antibodies made the proteins visible on scans, making early diagnosis – and life-saving treatment – possible.

In 2015, Krtin's discovery won him second prize in the Google Science Fair's Scientific Innovator category. Since then, Krtin has also invented a method to treat a particularly deadly form of breast cancer, another amazing idea that could one day save thousands of lives.

> "Coming up with the idea itself, anyone can do that – it is just whether you want to go for it."

STEM Prodigies Through History

Throughout history, children and teenagers have put their curious minds and passion for new ideas to the test in the fields of science, technology, engineering and mathematics (STEM), often with groundbreaking results.

1824 Louis Braille (1809–1852) was blinded in an accident as a child. So at fifteen he created braille, a writing and reading system for the blind and visually impaired that is still in use today.

1642 The French mathematician and inventor **Blaise Pascal** (1623–1662) was a genius. By eighteen, while working for his accountant father, he had invented the mechanical calculator: the first working calculator of its type. Blaise also invented the hydraulic press, the syringe and probability theory (using maths to predict the chance of something happening). A unit of pressure, a computer programming language and several mathematical and scientific laws are named after him.

1898 The Indian mathematician and child genius **Srinivasa Ramanujan** (1887–1920) had taught himself college-level mathematics by age eleven. By thirteen, he'd mastered trigonometry (a type of mathematics that calculates the lengths and angles of triangles) and produced several important mathematical theories. He also solved many previously unsolvable mathematical problems before adulthood.

1921 American electrical engineer **Philo T. Farnsworth** (1906–1971) was just fourteen when he invented the image dissector, a machine that used electric signals to send pictures. This later led to the invention of the electronic television.

1968 **Bill Gates** (1955–), the co-founder of Microsoft and one of the richest men in the world, created his first software program – a version of tic-tac-toe – on a school computer when he was just thirteen years old.

2010 At twelve, India's **Priyanshi Somani** (1998–) was the youngest participant in the Mental Calculation World Cup. She went on to win the title, beating thirty-six other competitors, many of them adults. In five Mental Calculation World Cups, she is the only participant to have achieved a one hundred per cent score in addition, multiplication and square root.

1980 The UK's **Ruth Lawrence** (1971–) was nine when she passed her O-level and A-level pure mathematics exams. By age thirteen she had completed a bachelor's degree at Oxford, becoming the youngest person in modern times to graduate from the university. After earning a bachelor's degree in physics and a PhD in mathematics, Ruth became a junior fellow at Harvard University in Boston, USA, at just nineteen. She continues her work as a professor of mathematics today.

2004 At nine years old, Pakistan's **Arfa Abdul Karim Randhawa** (1995–2012) became the youngest-ever Microsoft Certified Professional (an honour earned by passing exams in the use of Microsoft programs), a title she retained until 2008.

2008 At just fourteen, the American scientist and engineer **Taylor Wilson** (1994–) became the youngest person to build a nuclear fusion reactor (a complex machine that creates energy when atoms are fused together).

Marita Cheng

1989– | ENGINEER | AUSTRALIA

Marita Cheng was determined to use her passion for engineering to make a difference. In 2007, she created Nudge, an app that reminded patients to take their medication. Nudge won first prize at the University of Melbourne Entrepreneurship Challenge and was later sold in chemists' shops across the city. Then, upon seeing that her university engineering class was mostly boys, Marita made it her mission to inspire more girls to become scientists.

In 2008 she founded Robogals, which runs robotics workshops for schoolgirls around the world. In celebration of her achievements, Marita was named 2012's Australian of the Year. But her work had only just begun: the following year she founded 2Mar Robotics (now aubot), which builds robots that help sick and injured people in their homes. Marita continues to prove that science and engineering are not only fun, but they can transform people's lives.

Jacob Barnett

1998– | MATHEMATICIAN | USA

When doctors told Katherine Barnett that her two-year-old son, Jacob, had severe autism and would probably never learn to speak, she worried for his future. But she soon noticed that Jacob was happiest when solving complex puzzles and maths problems. It was then she decided to home-school her son so that he could focus on his passions.

In just two weeks, Jacob had completed the high-school maths curriculum. At ten, he was accepted to Purdue University, Indiana, USA, to study astrophysics and work on his scientific theories. Five years later, Jacob won a place at Canada's Perimeter Institute for Theoretical Physics, becoming the youngest-ever student to study for a PhD at the world-famous research centre. You can be sure that Jacob has a bright future ahead of him.

FILM AND MUSIC

Have you ever dreamed of performing on stage in front of thousands of cheering fans or writing pop songs that sell millions around the world? Perhaps you see yourself on the big screen, as a high-kicking superhero or a wand-waving wizard? Maybe you have a passion for classical music and aspire to become one of the greatest musicians of your generation? If all this seems like a long way off, take a look at the children in this section – every one of them is proof that, through talent, hard work and a whole lot of determination, it is possible to make your childhood dreams come true.

Some, like Justin Bieber, Taylor Swift and Zara Larsson, have been topping the charts and rocking the stage since their early teens. Others, like Quvenzhané Wallis, Daniel Radcliffe and Chloë Grace Moretz, have become some of the best-loved child film actors of all time. Then there are Ziyu He, Alex Prior and Nobuyuki Tsujii, new icons of classical music.

But success on such a grand scale does not come easy. It takes thousands of hours of practice, endless dedication and often a stroke of luck to make it to the top. But if you live for music, love singing or adore acting, perhaps you also have what it takes to reach for the stars?

Ziyu He

1999– | VIOLINIST | CHINA

Ziyu He was five when he picked up a violin for the first time. He has since grown to become one of the world's finest violinists. Born in Qingdao, China, Ziyu was invited to study violin at Salzburg's International Summer Academy. The entire family moved to Austria, with Ziyu's career going from strength to strength.

In 2014, he won first place in the Eurovision Young Musicians competition. Then, in 2016 he won the grandest prize of all: first place in the Menuhin competition, the world's leading contest for violinists.

Ziyu added another string to his bow when he played Bartók's Second Violin Concerto with the world-famous Vienna Philharmonic Orchestra, making him one of the youngest soloists ever to perform with the group. Today, Ziyu continues to share his remarkable gift on grand stages around the world.

Quvenzhané Wallis

2003– | ACTOR | USA

The actress Quvenzhané Wallis was just six years old when she starred in the 2012 film *Beasts of the Southern Wild*. Quvenzhané played Hushpuppy, a girl who survives a raging storm in the backwoods of Louisiana, USA. Not only did her performance win her rave reviews but she also became the youngest-ever nominee for a Best Actress Oscar at the age of nine. Although she didn't win the Academy Award, she did win eighteen other awards. Those, along with the film's prizes from several international film festivals, made Quvenzhané a global superstar.

Next, the actress appeared in the Oscar-winning film *12 Years a Slave* before playing the title role in the remake of *Annie* the musical. Today, Quvenzhané is also a fashion model for Armani Junior, which suits her just fine – as long as she gets to wear her favourite colour, pink!

Daniel Radcliffe

1989– | ACTOR | UK

It took eleven-year-old actor Daniel Radcliffe eight months and many auditions to win the role that would make him a star. Nowadays it would be hard to imagine anyone else as Hogwarts' favourite young wizard, Harry Potter. Although it was Harry who made him famous, Daniel had already appeared in 2001's *The Tailor of Panama* and the BBC's *David Copperfield*. His role in *David Copperfield* drew the attention of producer David Heyman, who was searching for the perfect actor to play the boy wizard. With filming for the *Harry Potter* series set to take place in Los Angeles, USA, Daniel's parents turned down the role at first. But thankfully the film shoot moved to the UK, and the stage was set for eleven-year-old Daniel to make movie magic.

Harry Potter and the Philosopher's Stone was released in 2001 to spellbound audiences. Millions of fans fell in love with the enchanting trio – Daniel, Emma Watson (as Hermione) and Rupert Grint (as Ron) – at the heart of the story. In fact, *Harry Potter and the Deathly Hallows – Part 2*, the final film in the series, became not only the highest-earning *Harry Potter* movie but also one of only thirty films ever to earn over $1 billion at the box office.

Despite his enormous success, Daniel never took his fame for granted. While still in his teens, he enrolled in acting classes to stretch his skills. Since then he has starred in a range of films, including a horror (2012's *The Woman in Black*), a thriller (2013's *Kill Your Darlings*) and a sci-fi fantasy (2015's *Victor Frankenstein*), while he has also won several awards for his theatre work. From child star to serious actor, there is little doubt that Daniel will be entertaining audiences for many years to come.

"If you can wake up every day and be emotionally open and honest regardless of what you get back from the world then you can be the hero of your own story."

Taylor Swift

1989– | SINGER-SONGWRITER AND MUSICIAN | USA

Taylor Swift is a force of nature. In just over a decade she has sold a staggering 40 million albums, had a string of hits and transformed from country singer into pop princess. She has ten Grammy Awards, nineteen American Music Awards and twenty-one *Billboard* Music Awards, and has been honoured in just about every artistic category. Add to this the fact that Taylor is one of the twenty-first century's best songwriters, a fashion icon and an idol to millions, and you get one stellar all-singing, all-songwriting superstar!

Even as a child Taylor's passion for music was obvious. At ten she was singing in contests and at fairs in Pennsylvania, USA, where she grew up. By twelve she had learned to play guitar and was writing her own songs. The following year the Swift family moved to Nashville, Tennessee – otherwise known as "Music City" – to take Taylor's career to the next level. Within a year she had signed a record deal. The girl from small-town America was about to hit the big time.

In 2006, Taylor released her debut album, with the single "Our Song" topping the US country music chart. Then, in 2008, Taylor's second album *Fearless* hit number one on both the US country and pop charts, proof that both country and pop fans adored her music. *Fearless* was named Album of the Year at the Grammy Awards, making twenty-year-old Taylor the youngest-ever artist to win the award.

> "I didn't want to just be another girl singer. I wanted there to be something that set me apart."

By the time of *1989*'s release in 2014, Taylor had become a fully fledged pop star, with the singles "Shake it Off", "Bad Blood" and "Blank Space" all topping the US *Billboard* Hot 100. Taylor once again made music history when she won the Grammy Album of the Year for a second time, making her the first female artist in music history to win twice!

The records kept on coming with the release of Taylor's sixth studio album, 2017's *Reputation*. The video for "Look What You Made Me Do" got more views in twenty-four hours than any other video in history. Not only did the track hit number one in the USA but it was also Taylor's first UK number one.

So what is it that sets Taylor apart from other musicians? As a songwriter, not only can she produce hits but she also connects with her fans through her deeply personal lyrics. She is a sensational performer on stage and a clever businesswoman off stage. Taylor also has a huge heart – she has donated millions to hospitals, charities and children's education, and is a role model to her fans around the world. Still only in her twenties, Taylor has proved that above all else, it is important to be courageous and kind, and stay true to yourself.

Nobuyuki Tsujii

1988– | PIANIST AND COMPOSER | JAPAN

Those lucky enough to have seen Nobuyuki Tsujii in concert have often been moved to tears. The Japanese pianist has mastered many of the most difficult classical pieces in history, performing them with breathtaking ease. But what makes Nobuyuki's achievements even more extraordinary is that he was born blind. Music scores are available in braille, but Nobuyuki learns music by ear.

At age two, Nobuyuki was playing "Do Re Mi" by ear on a toy piano. At seven he was winning top competitions and by ten he had played his first public concerto. Noboyuki is also a composer, with several albums and a Japan Film Critics Award for film scores to his name.

Already a superstar in his home country, "Nobu Fever" is taking over and the "boy with the magic touch" is capturing people's hearts around the world.

Zara Larsson

1997– | SINGER | SWEDEN

In 2008, when ten-year-old Zara Larsson took to the stage in Sweden's version of *Britain's Got Talent*, she wowed the audience and judges alike with her incredible voice. Then, when Zara was crowned winner, a star was born. By fourteen, the singer had signed her first record deal and released her debut album, *Introducing*. The single "Uncover" shot to number one in Sweden and Norway, making Zara a superstar in Scandinavia. But bigger and better things were yet to come…

In 2013, Zara signed a deal with the US record label Epic and released her album *1* the following year. In 2016 "Lush Life" and "Girls Like" appeared in the UK Top Ten at the same time. Since then, she has supported her idol Beyoncé on tour, and with fans all over the world, the stage is set for Zara Larsson: global superstar.

Alex Prior

1992– | CONDUCTOR AND COMPOSER | UK

Alex Prior dislikes the phrase "child prodigy". Instead, he credits his extraordinary talent and achievements in classical music to hard work, confidence and a deep passion for the arts.

Born to a British father and a Russian mother, Alex began playing the piano and composing at eight. As a youngster he attended weekend classes at the Royal College of Music in London. But his musical gifts soon outgrew those of his peers and he decided to aim even higher. By seventeen, he had earned two masters degrees from the Saint Petersburg Conservatory, becoming the youngest student since the great Russian composer Sergei Prokofiev to graduate from the music school with distinction in conducting. Since then, Alex has gone on to conduct in some of the world's best concert halls.

In 2010, Alex became an assistant to guest conductors at the Seattle Symphony, one of the USA's top orchestras. The following year he was asked to compose original works for the Royal Danish Ballet and the Los Angeles Opera. In fact, he has composed more than forty symphonies, operas and ballets – and all this before reaching his twenties!

In 2016, Alex was chosen to lead Canada's Edmonton Symphony Orchestra. His talent, drive and passion make him the perfect person for the role. As chief conductor he is responsible for creating a programme that not only celebrates Canada's musical history, but also inspires and encourages more young people to fall in love with classical music.

"I worked very hard at a very young age ... but it really does feel like it's paying off ... I get to go on stage and make music with friends and colleagues."

Film and Music Prodigies Through History

Throughout history, gifted children have made their mark on film and music. From talented toddlers who learn to play an instrument before they can walk, to singing sensations and amazing actors, these junior superstars are proof that you can win fans at any age.

1826 Germany's **Clara Schumann** (1819–1896) had mastered the piano by age seven and was composing by ten. She went on to play more than 1,300 concerts in her career.

1908 The Chilean classical pianist **Claudio Arrau** (1903–1991) read music before he could read words. He gave his first concert at five and became one of the greatest pianists of the twentieth century.

1759 Wolfgang Amadeus Mozart (1756–1791) is the most famous child prodigy of all time. He began playing the harpsichord when he was just three, started composing music at age five and wrote his first symphony at eight. As a young boy, he travelled with his parents across Europe, performing in royal courts and grand concert halls. Sometimes the Austrian musician would even play the piano blindfolded! Mozart died at thirty-five, but during his short life he composed over 600 pieces, including some of the most celebrated in history.

1778 The British composer **William Crotch** (1775–1847) was just three and a half years old when he played the organ for King George III. It is said that he wrote the "Westminster Quarters", the bell chimes that the clock in Big Ben rings every fifteen minutes.

1932 **Shirley Temple** (1928–2014) was just three when she began her film career, starring in films like *Bright Eyes* (1934), *Curly Top* (1935) and *Heidi* (1937). The actress, singer and dancer, known for her blond curls and sparkling smile, was also the first child star to be awarded a special Juvenile Academy Award in 1935, at six. Shirley starred in over forty films before retiring at age twenty-two.

1961 R&B/soul singer **Stevie Wonder** (1950–) was signed to Tamla Motown Records at eleven. At thirteen, he became the youngest artist ever to top the US *Billboard* 100 music charts, with the song "Fingertips". He is now known as one of the twentieth century's greatest musicians.

1974 The USA's **Tatum O'Neal** (1963–) became the youngest person ever to win an Oscar when she won the Best Supporting Actress award at age ten, for her role in *Paper Moon*.

1997 Country/pop singer **LeAnn Rimes** (1982–) became the youngest person to ever win a Grammy award when she won the Best New Artist and Best Female Country Vocal Performance trophies at age fourteen.

1964 **Michael Jackson** (1958–2009) is the biggest superstar in music history. When Michael was six, he and his four elder brothers had a string of hits as the Jackson 5. Michael had even bigger success as a solo artist. In 1982, he released *Thriller*, which has sold around 65 million copies, making it the best-selling album of all time. He was also famous for his unforgettable voice and sensational dancing, especially his signature move the "Moonwalk". Sadly Michael died aged just fifty, but he will forever be remembered as the "King of Pop".

1963 The Chinese-American cellist **Yo-Yo Ma** (1955–) performed for President John F. Kennedy at age seven. He has since recorded more than ninety albums and won eighteen Grammy awards.

2006 India's **Kishan Shrikanth** (1996–) became the youngest director of a feature film, *Care of Footpath*, at nine. He also wrote the script for his film, which was dubbed into five Indian languages and translated into English.

Chloë Grace Moretz

1997– | ACTOR | USA

Even as a youngster, American movie star Chloë Grace Moretz stunned both filmmakers and audiences with her mature acting style. Whether she's playing a slick superhero (2010's *Kick-Ass*), a young vampire (2010's *Let Me In*), or voicing a fairytale princess (2018's *Red Shoes & The Seven Dwarfs*), Chloë Grace takes every role seriously. For *Kick-Ass*, a then thirteen-year-old Chloë Grace trained with martial arts master Jackie Chan for three months before filming, and performed most of her own stunts.

Despite winning rave reviews and working with some of Hollywood's biggest directors, Chloë Grace has managed to stay grounded, allowing her terrific talent to shine.

Justin Bieber

1994– | SINGER-SONGWRITER | CANADA

There are very few people in the world who haven't heard of Justin Bieber. The Canadian pop star has topped the charts for almost a decade, while the media, 100 million Twitter followers and Justin's loyal "Beliebers" watch his every move.

Justin learned to play guitar, drums, trumpet and piano as a child. But it was when he began posting videos of his singing to YouTube that his career took off. Within a year he'd signed a record deal. With the release of his 2010 single "Baby" Justin won millions of instant fans around the world.

Megahit after megahit followed and in 2016 Justin became the first artist in UK history to have his songs chart at numbers 1, 2 and 3 at the same time. But Justin is more than just a singing superstar: through the Make-A-Wish Foundation he has fulfilled almost 300 "wishes" for terminally ill children, making him the heart-throb with a heart of gold.

ENVIRONMENT

The environment is everything in the world around us – the air we breathe, the water we drink and bathe in, and the ground below us. We are lucky to live on a planet that has stunning natural beauty, magnificent wildlife and precious resources. But today, many of the wonders that make our world so special are under threat. Climate change is heating the planet and people are fleeing from environmental disasters, such as drought, floods and hurricanes. The human population is growing quickly – from 1 billion in the year 1800 to a possible 8.4 billion by the mid-2030s. The world's wild habitats and oceans are suffering due to deforestation, overfishing and pollution.

But there is hope! Activists and non-profit organizations are fighting for environmental causes, while governments are making laws to reduce mankind's impact on the planet. Ordinary people like you and me can also make a big difference, by recycling and using less water and power.

And as the children in this section prove, you're never too young to start! Kids like Olivia Bouler, Birke Baehr and Ken Amante have channelled their passion into causes close to their hearts. Boyan Slat has come up with a potential solution to save the world's oceans from poisonous plastics. Maritza Morales Casanova, Misimi Isimi and Ta'Kaiya Blaney are committed to educating other young people about the environmental issues in their communities, while Tom Youngman and Kehkashan Basu speak on behalf of the world's youth at leading environmental summits.

No matter their method, each of these children is driven by a desire to build a sustainable future for generations to come. Hopefully their stories will inspire you to follow their lead.

Maritza Morales Casanova

1984– | ENVIRONMENTAL ACTIVIST | MEXICO

Mexico's beautiful Yucatán Peninsula lies between the Caribbean Sea and the Gulf of Mexico. This ancient land of tropical jungles and sandy beaches was once home to the Mayan civilization, whose people built temples to their gods that still stand today. But like many other fragile environments around the world, the Yucatán is in danger. Climate change and a growing population are threatening to destroy its precious natural resources.

At the age of ten, Maritza Morales Casanova had a dream: that some day her people would live in harmony with the environment, just as their predecessors, the Ancient Mayans, had done. Knowing that local communities were often too poor to spend money on environmental education, Maritza took it upon herself to make a change. In 1995 she launched Humanity United to Nature in Harmony for Beauty, Welfare and Goodness (HUNAB). At first she taught friends and neighbours how to grow plants and care for animals. By thirteen, she was campaigning for land and funds to build an education centre, so that she could reach even more children across the Yucatán. Next, Maritza studied environmental planning and conservation at university, to back up her goals.

After devoting almost twenty years to the cause, Maritza's dream finally came true: the Ceiba Pentandra park opened its doors in 2013. Now, thousands of young people come to the park each year to learn how to care for the environment in classes run by children, for children. By sharing the lessons of the Mayan past, Maritza believes that these youngsters will grow up to become the environmental stewards of the future.

"To me, everyone who is born in the Yucatán has a drop of Mayan blood, and this provides us with the vision and commitment to our Grandmother Earth."

Olivia Bouler

2000– | ENVIRONMENTAL ARTIST | CANADA

On 20th April 2010, tragedy struck the Deepwater Horizon oil rig, just 66km (41 miles) off the US coast. A fire caused a massive explosion and millions of litres of oil spilled into the Gulf of Mexico. Within days, an enormous oil slick had swallowed precious coastal habitats and was threatening marine wildlife, including many seabird species.

When eleven-year-old Olivia Bouler heard about the disaster she wept, then resolved to do everything she could to help. She had the idea to paint pictures of her favourite birds, sell the prints and donate the money she raised to the Audubon Society, a conservation organization whose volunteers were leading the clean-up and rescue. Olivia's beautiful bird paintings went on to raise nearly $200,000 for affected birdlife, proving that just one person can make a big difference.

Tom Youngman

1993– | YOUTH ACTIVIST | UK

Tom Youngman believes that young people everywhere can play a part in protecting Planet Earth. He is committed to showing children that not only can they make a difference in their local communities but at government level, too.

At fourteen, Tom co-founded Green Vision, a youth group dedicated to environmental action in Bath, England. Its activities included Guerrilla Gardening (planting gardens and vegetable patches on wasteland) and a People's Kitchen scheme (preparing cheap or free meals from food that would otherwise have been thrown away).

In 2010, Tom was selected to join a government Youth Advisory Panel. In his role he worked with politicians and leading environmental organizations to give young people a say in shaping government policy. Now a graduate, Tom remains committed to tackling climate change by working with several eco-groups in both Spain and the UK.

Boyan Slat

1994– | FOUNDER OF THE OCEAN CLEAN-UP | THE NETHERLANDS

Did you know that the oceans cover more than seventy per cent of our planet's surface? That's a lot of water! Surely that's enough to sustain humans and marine wildlife for centuries to come? Sadly it may not be: more waste than ever before is being dumped into the oceans, threatening this delicate ecosystem and the wildlife – and people – that depend on it for survival.

Boyan Slat loves to dive. As a teenager he spent his spare time beneath the ocean waves, hoping to catch a glimpse of a shoal of fish or maybe a shark. But in 2011, while Boyan was diving in Greece, he barely saw any fish. Instead, he found masses of floating plastic bags. When he returned to the Netherlands he decided to research the effects of plastic pollution for a school science project. He discovered that humans produce more than 300 million tonnes of plastic each year, large amounts of which end up in the ocean. It came as a shock, but in that moment Boyan had found his life's mission.

By the age of eighteen, Boyan had come up with a method to remove plastic from the ocean on a grand scale. His idea was to create an enormous floating system, with filters forming a huge "net". Ocean currents would push the plastic into this trap, where it could be removed from the water. It was an ambitious plan – many people said it wouldn't work, but Boyan was determined to prove them wrong. He struggled for years to secure sponsorship, but when his TED Talk went viral, the offers of help began flooding in. Finally,

in 2013, Boyan founded the Ocean Clean-Up, a team of scientists and researchers who would help him in his quest.

Since then, the Ocean Clean-Up team has researched and developed new technologies – including Boyan's floating system – which it hopes will rid the ocean of plastic. And for its first major clean-up operation, the team has the Great Pacific Garbage Patch in its sights.

This swirling mass of plastic is trapped between powerful ocean currents in the northern Pacific. Some environmentalists estimate it to be twice the size of Texas, the second-largest state of the USA! Such a colossal amount of debris is causing serious damage to the ocean ecosystem. Sea birds, sea turtles and marine mammals, such as dolphins and whales, end up eating the

plastic and dying. Fish ingest the plastic's deadly toxins, and if humans go on to consume these fish, they can end up ingesting the toxins too.

In 2016, the Ocean Clean-Up team made the first aerial search of the Garbage Patch, aiming to test Boyan's floating clean-up system in these waters in 2018 and reduce the patch by half its size within five years. Not only will this have an enormous impact on the future of the oceans but Boyan will be one step closer to achieving his dream: swimming among the fish in plastic-free oceans.

"It's in my nature that when people say something is impossible I like to prove them wrong."

Kehkashan Basu

2000– | YOUTH AMBASSADOR | UAE

World Environment Day happens every year on 5th June, the day that Kehkashan Basu was born. As such, she believes it is her destiny to protect Planet Earth.

As Youth Ambassador for the World Future Council, she encourages young people to commit to a more sustainable future. At twelve she became the youngest person to address Rio+20, the UN Conference on Sustainable Development, while in 2016 she was awarded the International Children's Peace Prize.

Kehkashan is also the founder of Green Hope (UAE), a youth organization that runs hundreds of environmental projects, from tree planting to beach clean-ups. Green Hope has since gone global, with around 3,000 children now taking part in the group's activities.

Kehkashan is staying true to her cause. Each year on her birthday she plants a tree – a symbol of commitment to fulfilling her mission, one tree at a time.

Birke Baehr

1999– | YOUTH ADVOCATE | USA

Birke Baehr is on a quest: to educate children about the benefits of sustainable food and agriculture. At nine, he began investigating the way food is mass-produced. He learned that often chemicals are used to stop pests damaging crops, while millions of cattle and other livestock are kept in dark, confined spaces. To Birke, not only do these conditions affect the food that ends up on our plates but they also damage the environment.

Birke soon began volunteering at organic farms in his spare time. From composting to using organic pesticides made from safe, natural sources, these farms prove that food can be produced in a more sustainable way. By sharing this knowledge with young people and their families around the world, Birke believes he can help them make the right food choices – both for themselves and the environment.

Ken Amante

2005– | ANIMAL ACTIVIST | PHILIPPINES

Stray animals are a common sight in the Philippines: they live alone on the streets, often fall sick and scavenge for food to survive. However, many people are doing their best to help, including Ken Amante.

Ken always loved animals – even as a toddler he would sleep with his father's pet cat, Hajime-kun, every night. But while out walking his dog one day, he came across three strays. The dogs were extremely thin and had mange, a contagious skin disease. Rather than being scared, Ken felt an overwhelming need to help. The strays were far too nervous for him to pet, but each day Ken bought tins of dog food with his pocket money and returned to feed them. After several weeks the dogs began to trust Ken. Finally, he was able to bring them home to start the long road to recovery.

In 2014, Ken's dad uploaded pictures to the internet of his son helping the strays. Within days. the images went viral and Ken received hundreds of donations from animal lovers around the world. The nine-year-old decided to use the money to open an animal shelter in his hometown, Davao City.

Since then, Happy Animals Club has rescued hundreds of cats and dogs from city streets. The club provides its animals with a safe home, high-quality food and vet care. Ken and his father are now helped by volunteers, and Ken's ambition is to raise funds to open many more shelters. This little boy with a huge heart is proof that a simple act of kindness really can change the world.

10 Ways to Make a Difference to the Environment!

The very first Earth Day was held in the USA on 22nd April 1970. Earth Day is now held every year on 22nd April and billions of people from around the world take part. Schools, communities, charities and environmental organizations from more than 180 countries get involved in thousands of different events to raise environmental awareness and push for change. You can learn more about getting involved in Earth Day at this website: www.earthday.org. But if you can't find an event near you, don't worry – there are lots of small things you can do every day to make a difference.

1  Turn off lights and electronic gadgets when you're not using them, to save energy.

2 Avoid long showers, to save water.

3  Ask your parents if you can walk or cycle to school, rather than going by car.

4 Organize a litter pick of your local park or school grounds.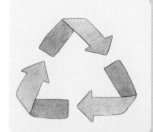

5  Volunteer at your local nature reserve for the day.

6 Swap plastic disposable water bottles for reusable ones to avoid waste.

7  When out hiking, stay on marked trails to avoid disturbing plant and animal life.

8 Don't throw away perfectly good unwanted gifts – donate them to a charity shop instead!

9  Plant a flower garden for bees and butterflies to enjoy.

10 Save water by turning off the tap when you're brushing your teeth.

Misimi Isimi

2008– | ENVIRONMENTALIST | NIGERIA

Misimi Isimi may only be small, but she has an enormous passion for the environment. With her mother's support, at the age of just eight Misimi founded the Eco-kids green club in her home country, Nigeria. As president of the club, Misimi tours local schools, giving talks that encourage other children to "go green" and live sustainably.

Misimi is also an ambassador to environmental organizations in other African countries, including Young Planter Initiative in Uganda. The group aims to plant a million trees in a year in areas where logging and industry have destroyed the forest. Somehow Misimi manages to fit all this in around her schoolwork!

In 2017, Misimi was honoured at the Africa Clean-up Awards as the "first passionate child environmentalist in Nigeria". She is now working on launching an environmental comic for kids and hopes that other children will discover a passion for the environment as enormous as hers.

Ta'Kaiya Blaney

2001– | ENVIRONMENTALIST | CANADA

Ta'Kaiya Blaney is from the Tla'amin First Nation, one of 634 indigenous communities in Canada. She grew up among the lakes, rivers and mountains of British Columbia. But even here, in one of the most beautiful places on Earth, industries such as oil and mining threaten the delicate ecosystem.

At the age of ten, Ta'Kaiya decided she had to do something to protect her homeland. In 2011, she released "Shallow Waters", a song she wrote about how oil spills damage marine wildlife. The song's video went viral and soon Ta'Kaiya was speaking and performing at environmental events around the world.

Today, Ta'Kaiya continues to dedicate her time to preserving indigenous lands. She hopes that by speaking out, she will encourage young people to join her in her mission to protect not only her community but also the Earth as a whole.

SPORT

Do you ever imagine what it would feel like to stand on the winners' podium at the Olympic Games or to lift a trophy at Wimbledon? Maybe you're a natural on the football pitch and you long to score the winning goal in the World Cup final. Or perhaps you dream of tackling the planet's biggest challenges, such as climbing Mount Everest or swimming the English Channel. If this sounds like you, then you could be on your way to sporting glory! But be prepared: it takes real commitment to become a champion. You'll need dedication, desire and drive to make it to the top. Endless hours of training are a must, while you also have to be mentally prepared for the testing times ahead.

But don't let the idea of all that hard work put you off – as the children in this section prove, taking part in sport of any kind can be rewarding. Not only will you get fit, make friends for life and have tons of fun along the way, you may also get the chance to represent your nation.

Take Pelé, Nadia Comaneci, Jahangir Khan and Michelle Kwan, sensational sportsmen and women who are not only superstars in their own countries but all over the world. Or maybe you could follow in the record-breaking footsteps of Jordan Romero, Martina Hingis and Lydia Ko? With great talent comes great responsibility: sometimes, like Yusra Mardini, your chosen sport could make you a hero.

Each of these children will hopefully inspire you to get off your sofa, get outside and get active. You may even discover that you have what it takes to become a sports star of the future.

Yusra Mardini

1998– | SWIMMER | SYRIA

Syria's Yusra Mardini is a talented swimmer with a remarkable past. By fourteen, she'd competed at the World Championships and was on course to a fantastic career.

But all that changed when her country faced civil war. In 2015, Yusra's family home was destroyed and she and her sister, Sarah, fled Syria for Turkey. From there they travelled to Greece in a boat carrying twenty people. But not long into the perilous journey, the boat's motor failed and they were stranded. With little chance of rescue, Yusra and Sarah jumped into the sea and pushed the boat for three and a half hours, swimming the refugees to safety.

The pair eventually made it to Germany where, at eighteen, Yusra was selected to represent the first-ever Refugee Olympic Team, going on to win the opening heat of the 100m butterfly at Rio in 2016. A true champion, Yusra is now a UN Refugee Agency Goodwill Ambassador.

Jahangir Khan

1963– | SQUASH PLAYER | PAKISTAN

When Pakistan's Jahangir Khan was a child, doctors said he was too weak to ever play sport. But Jahangir grew up in a family of squash players, and he was determined to prove the experts wrong.

After training for many years with his father and brother, fifteen-year-old Jahangir gained enough strength and skill to enter the 1979 World Amateur Individual Championship, becoming the competition's youngest-ever winner. Then, at seventeen he became the youngest-ever World Open Champion. But Jahangir wasn't done with breaking records – between 1981 and 1986 he won 555 matches in a row, the longest winning streak of any professional athlete in sport history!

Jahangir continued to dominate the game throughout his career, winning the World Open five more times and the British Open ten times. Doctors may have overlooked his potential as a boy, but through sheer dedication and belief, Jahangir became the greatest squash player of all time.

Pelé

1940– | FOOTBALLER | BRAZIL

Today, a handful of world-class footballers compete for the title of "Greatest Player on Earth". But in the 1960s and 1970s, there was no debate. The greatest footballer in the world was Pelé.

Edson Arantes do Nascimento grew up in poverty. His family couldn't afford a real football, so the young Brazilian, who was nicknamed Pelé as a schoolboy, would practise his favourite sport with a grapefruit or a sock stuffed with newspaper. Pelé's natural talent shone through, making him the star of several local youth teams. His big break came in 1956 when, at just fifteen, he signed to his first professional club, Santos. He immediately lived up to expectations, scoring in his debut game and becoming the league's top scorer that season!

Within a year, Pelé was selected to represent Brazil in the 1958 World Cup. Brazil – and Pelé – had a sensational championship. At seventeen years and 249 days old not only did Pelé become the youngest footballer ever to play in a World Cup final match but he also scored twice, helping Brazil to a 5–2 victory against host nation Sweden. His performance – including a hat trick against France in the semi-final – won him Young Player of the Tournament and made him a global icon.

For the rest of his career, Pelé created magic whenever he played. He is the most successful league-scorer in history, with 678 goals, while his speed, stamina and sheer power were unrivalled on the pitch. His flair and creative play won him millions of fans and three World Cup titles (the only player in history to achieve this). He was named Athlete of the Century and Footballer of the Century. To this day, he is still the greatest footballer the world has ever seen.

"Success is no accident. It is hard work, perseverance, learning, studying, sacrifice and most of all, love of what you are doing or learning to do."

Nadia Comaneci

1961– | GYMNAST | ROMANIA

Day Two of the 1976 Montreal Olympic Games, Canada. The stands in the Montreal Forum are packed for one of the games' most thrilling events: the women's uneven bars. As gymnast Nadia Comaneci takes to the floor in her white leotard, her glossy brown hair neatly tied with a matching ribbon, the crowd falls silent. Moments later, the fourteen-year-old leaps into action.

Nadia was born in Onești, a small Romanian town in the foothills of the Carpathian Mountains. She was such an active child that her mother decided to send her to gymnastics classes as a way for Nadia to let off steam. But the hobby soon became her passion. The famous gymnastics coach Béla Károlyi spotted the six-year-old doing cartwheels in the school playground and invited her to train at his new gymnastics school.

Nadia excelled under Béla's guidance. In 1970, she won the Romanian Nationals, becoming the youngest gymnast ever to win the competition at age nine. Within three years she had collected her first international gold medals, in the all-around, vault and uneven bars events, at the 1973 Junior Friendship Tournament. Then, at thirteen, she competed in the European Championships for the first time and won gold in every event except the floor exercise, in which she placed second. Little Nadia had become a national icon but now she was ready for Olympic glory.

The pressure was on at Montreal 1976 – Nadia's first Olympic Games. All eyes were on the girl in the white leotard as she leaped on to the uneven bars and performed a dazzling routine, which included two handstands and a flawless dismount. Everyone expected her to win gold, but no one could have predicted what would happen next. When the judges' scores flashed up on the board, the crowd went wild – Nadia had scored the first perfect 10 in Olympic history! It was such a special event that the official scoreboard couldn't even register the score – there was only room for three numbers up to 9.99. Her 10.00 had to be displayed as a 1.00!

Nadia's outstanding Olympics didn't end there: she went on to score six more perfect 10s in the competition and win three individual gold medals, a team silver and a bronze in the floor exercise, making her the star of the games. She also dominated at the 1980 Moscow Olympic Games, winning two more gold and two silver medals, before finally retiring from the sport in 1984.

So what is it that made Nadia such a special gymnast? Certainly she was famous for her perfect technique, but she was creative too. She was the first gymnast to successfully perform a number of moves, including the aerial walkover on the beam and the double-twist dismount on the bars – yet she always made it look so easy! Her performances changed the sport forever and inspired millions of young athletes. To them, she will always be the tiny champion who became a giant of gymnastics.

"Hard work has made it easy.
That is my secret. That is why I win."

47

Martina Hingis

1980– | TENNIS PLAYER | SWITZERLAND

Since turning professional at fourteen, Martina Hingis has won twenty-five Grand Slam titles! But the Swiss player is best known for her collection of "youngest-ever" records.

In 1993, twelve-year-old Martina claimed victory in the girls' singles championship at the French Open, becoming the youngest player ever to win a Grand Slam junior title. In 1996 she made history again when, at fifteen years and 282 days, she won the Wimbledon women's doubles title, becoming the youngest player ever to win a Grand Slam.

The records kept on coming – in 1997, Martina became both the youngest tennis player in the Open Era to win a Wimbledon singles title and the youngest-ever to be ranked World No. 1. Only a handful of players have reached all four Grand Slam finals in a single year, and she did it at sixteen! From child prodigy to champion, Martina is a true tennis legend.

Ricky Rubio

1990– | BASKETBALL PLAYER | SPAIN

Basketball's Ricky Rubio is a sensational sportsman. In 2005, at just fourteen, he became the youngest person ever to play in the Spanish basketball league. The following year, the junior Spanish national team won the International Basketball Federation's European Under-16 Championship. Ricky played so well that he was named Most Valuable Player of the tournament.

From there he signed to the EuroLeague and become, at sixteen, the first person born in the 1990s to play in the league. Ricky then made history again at the 2008 Beijing Olympics. The Spanish national team reached the last game of the tournament, making seventeen-year-old Ricky the youngest-ever person to play in an Olympic basketball final.

Today, Ricky plays point guard in the American NBA – the biggest basketball league in the world. As one of Spain's most celebrated athletes, Ricky is now hoping to steer his current team, the Utah Jazz, all the way to the NBA Finals.

Lydia Ko

1997– | GOLFER | NEW ZEALAND

Lydia Ko was always destined for greatness. She was five when she first picked up a golf club. By seven, she'd competed in her first golf competition – for adults! It was to be the first in a long line of major achievements.

As an amateur player, Lydia claimed victory in the 2012 Bing Lee/Samsung New South Wales Women's Open, making her the youngest person ever to win a professional golf tour competition. By 2014, seventeen-year-old Lydia was ready to join the Ladies Professional Golf Association (LPGA) tour. In April that year, she won her first LPGA tournament. Then in 2015 she broke another record – at seventeen years, nine months and nine days old she became World No. 1, making her the youngest player, male or female, to achieve that goal.

Lydia shows no signs of stopping. In 2016 she was named Young New Zealander of the Year in honour of her amazing career to date.

Jordan Romero

1996– | MOUNTAINEER | USA

When Jordan Romero saw a picture of the "Seven Summits" (the seven continents' highest mountains), he was inspired to climb them. Jordan's father and stepmother are experienced mountaineers; they helped him prepare for the enormous challenge ahead and accompanied him on his journeys.

By ten, Jordan had climbed the first peak – Africa's Mount Kilimanjaro. Four more peaks followed before it was time to tackle Mount Everest, the tallest mountain in the world at 8,848m (29,035ft). It would be a huge task – by that time, almost 220 climbers had already died on Everest's slopes. But seven days after setting off from base camp, thirteen-year-old Jordan became the youngest person ever to reach Everest's summit.

Then, at fifteen years, five months and twelve days, Jordan climbed Antarctica's Vinson Massif, becoming the youngest-ever person to climb all Seven Summits. But Jordan isn't finished – his next goal is to reach the highest point in all fifty US states.

Sports Prodigies Through History

From climbing the world's tallest mountain to clever tactics on the tennis court, young sportsmen and -women throughout history have proven they have what it takes to break records and win medals.

1868 At seventeen, **Tom Morris** (1851–1875) won the British Open, making him the youngest winner in the history of men's golf.

1896 Greek gymnast **Dimitrios Loundras** (1885–1970) is officially the youngest Olympian ever. He was just ten when he won bronze at the first modern Olympic games in Athens, Greece.

1989 Indian cricket star **Sachin Tendulkar** (1973–) played in his first International Test match at just sixteen years and 205 days old. He went on to become one of the world's greatest batsmen: he is the only player to have scored a hundred centuries in international matches. He holds the records for the highest number of runs scored in Test and One-Day International matches and he represented his nation's team for nearly twenty-four years.

1936 The American diver **Marjorie Gestring** (1922–1992) holds the record for youngest-ever person to win gold at the Summer Olympics. She was just thirteen years and 268 days old when she won the 3m springboard diving event in Berlin in 1936. Marjorie's record will probably never be beaten because the minimum age for Olympic participants is now sixteen.

1989 When US tennis player **Michael Chang** (1972–) won the French Open at just seventeen years and 110 days old, he became the youngest male winner of a tennis Grand Slam singles championship.

1994 When South Korea's **Kim Yun-Mi** (1980–) and her team claimed victory in the women's short track speed skating relay, she became the youngest athlete ever to win gold at the Winter Olympics, at thirteen years and eighty-three days old.

1995 At thirteen, **Dominique Moceanu** (1981–) became the youngest gymnast ever to win the senior all-around title at the US National Gymnastics Championships.

1998 On 11th February 1998, **Michael Owen** (1979–) became the youngest England football international of the twentieth century when he played in a game against Chile at eighteen years and fifty-nine days old. He is also the youngest player to have scored a hundred goals in the English Premier League.

2009 At fifteen, British diver **Tom Daley** (1994–) won gold in the individual 10m platform event at the International Swimming Federation World Championships. He went on to win two more Olympic bronzes, at the 2012 London Olympics and at Rio 2016.

2010 Chinese chess player **Hou Yifan** (1994–) became the youngest-ever women's World Chess Champion at sixteen.

2013 Chinese golfer **Guan Tianlang** (1998–) became the youngest player in history to compete in a PGA Tour when, aged fourteen, he qualified for the 2013 Masters Tournament.

2014 India's **Malavath Purna** (2000–) became the youngest-ever female, at thirteen years and eleven months, to climb Mount Everest.

2016 At eighteen, **Max Verstappen** (1997–) of the Netherlands became the youngest driver to win a Formula One race (the Spanish Grand Prix).

2000 Swimmer **Michael Phelps** (1985–) was just fifteen when he represented the USA in the Sydney 2000 Olympics, making him the youngest US Olympic team member since 1932. The following year Michael set the first of hundreds of world records in the 200m butterfly event at the World Aquatics Championships. He was the youngest male ever to set a swimming world record, at just fifteen years and nine months. Michael also became the first athlete to win eight gold medals at a single Olympic games (Beijing 2008), while he now has more Olympic medals (twenty-eight) than any other athlete in history.

2017 At fourteen, Japan's **Sota Fujii** (2002-), the youngest-ever professional shogi player (a Japanese version of chess), set the all-time record for games unbeaten when he won twenty-nine shogi matches in a row.

Michelle Kwan

1980– | FIGURE SKATER | USA

Michelle Kwan is one of the most famous figure skaters in history. During a sparkling career, she was crowned World Champion five times and US Champion nine times, while her grace and artistry on the ice are unrivalled.

Michelle grew up in a skating family – her brother was an ice-hockey player while her sister was also a top figure skater. At five years old, Michelle followed her siblings on to the ice and the following year won her first competition. By the age of eight, she was training three to four hours a day, fitting in practice around her schoolwork. The long hours at the rink were starting to become expensive for Michelle's parents, but thankfully for the young skater – and her fans – the Los Angeles Figure Skating Club recognized her potential and sponsored her training.

Michelle's professional career got off to a flying start. At eleven, she came ninth in the 1992 junior level US Championships. Two years later Michelle entered her first major international competition, the World Juniors, and won.

As Michelle skated her way to the top, her style matured. She developed strength and skill, and became known for her elegance, including her signature move the "change of edge" spiral. When combined, these talents made her unstoppable and in 1996, sixteen-year-old Michelle won both the US and World Skating Championships for the first time.

But it wasn't always easy. Michelle faced injuries, stumbled in several competitions and missed out on an Olympic gold medal. However, setbacks often make great champions stronger. Her performances continued to delight skating fans around the world. By the end of her career, Michelle had fulfilled her destiny as one of the greatest female figure skaters of all time.

"Winning is not about how many medals you get – it's about accomplishing goals and just being the best you can be!"

BUSINESS

Do you have new ideas all the time? Would you have the drive and determination to turn your idea into a fully fledged business? Are you passionate, full of energy and open to trying new things? If so, you may just have the makings of a young entrepreneur.

In this section of the book, you'll learn about nine young entrepreneurs who have taken the business world by storm. Mikaila Ulmer and Fraser Doherty each saw a problem and came up with a solution to fix it. Lily Born, Mabel Suglo and Mateusz Mach were guided by their desire to help others. George Burgess and Jordan Casey have transformed technology, while Tavi Gevinson and Mark Zuckerberg built empires from their bedrooms. No matter how they got there, all of these children are proof of one thing – being young won't stop you from finding success in business.

Running a business can be exciting but daunting. You must be prepared to work long hours and sacrifice your spare time to bring your ideas to life. You'll also need to be strong. You may stumble along the way, and you'll need the confidence to get up and carry on. It can also be hard to get adults to take you seriously, so you must have faith in your own abilities. But you don't have to go it alone. Most new entrepreneurs have help from their parents, teachers or mentors on their way to the top.

So if you like the idea of being your own boss or you have an idea that you think could change the world, always remember one thing: as long as you stay true to yourself and your values, success is within your grasp.

Lily Born

2003– | INVENTOR | USA

KANGAROO CUP!

CREATE!

Parkinson's disease is a condition that causes certain cells in the brain to deteriorate, or stop working over time. Patients develop tremors (shaking) and problems with balance, and this can lead to them losing the ability to control movement. The condition affects around 10 million people worldwide, including Lily Born's grandfather.

Eight-year-old Lily was inspired to help when she saw her grandfather's tremors made him spill his drinks. She couldn't stop his tremors … but she could change his cup! Lily built a test design, which featured three legs for stability and a curved rim that stopped any splashes. She named it the Kangaroo Cup because it reminded her of a kangaroo, which uses its tail as a "third leg" for stability. Lily's father was so impressed with the design that he encouraged her to pursue it. Together, they set up a Kickstarter campaign and raised $6,000 in donations.

The next step was to create a ceramic version of the cup. Ceramic is a cheap, easy-to-use material but it isn't perfect, as it breaks easily. Although the first design had some success, what Lily and her father really needed was a plastic version. However, building items from plastic is expensive – a huge team of experts is needed to operate specialized machinery. But Lily had come a long way and she wasn't about to quit now. She returned to Kickstarter and ended up raising over $60,000 to build a plastic version that would be stronger, easy to stack and – best of all – virtually impossible to break.

Since then, Lily has sold thousands of Kangaroo Cups and donates part of the profits to Parkinson's charities. Through determination and passion, she was able to turn her simple idea into a life-changing invention.

"Just because you're a kid, doesn't mean you can't do big and great things."

Mikaila Ulmer

2005– | CEO | USA

Being stung twice in one week might be enough to put anyone off bees for life, but not Mikaila Ulmer. Bees are an essential part of the food chain but they are under threat. So when Mikaila's great-grandmother sent her an old family recipe for flaxseed lemonade, the little girl spotted her chance to raise money for the organizations working to save bees.

With her parents' help, four-year-old Mikaila made her first batch of Me & the Bees Lemonade, using honey from local beekeepers. The lemonade created a buzz – soon the organic food chain Whole Foods began stocking it in stores around the USA. At the age of eleven, Mikaila also appeared on 'Shark Tank', a TV show for aspiring entrepreneurs, securing $60,000 in investment.

Today, Mikaila continues to donate part of her profits to bee foundations and beekeepers, while being a middle-school CEO keeps her as busy as a bee!

George Burgess

1992– | SOFTWARE ENTREPRENEUR | UK

While studying for his A-levels, George Burgess had a brainwave: why not make an app that would make exam revision faster and easier? With the help of his geography teacher – who became his first business adviser – George created EducationApps, a software company that builds apps and digital study guides for high school and college students.

Later, while at university, George secured over $1 million in investment for his business, which he relaunched as Gojimo in 2014. His team began working with teachers, professors and book publishers to create more than 60,000 questions in a hundred subjects, ranging from geography to German.

Since then Gojimo's apps have been downloaded over 500,000 times, while George left university to concentrate on his company full time. But even though he's no longer in school, George is still top of the class – in 2016, *Forbes* magazine named him one of the UK's best young entrepreneurs.

Tavi Gevinson

1996– | WRITER, EDITOR AND ACTOR | USA

When eleven-year-old Tavi Gevinson uploaded her first post to her fashion blog, *Style Rookie*, she hoped to gain followers who liked the same things she did. But instead, the young writer from Chicago, USA, became an internet superstar. Within a decade, Tavi went from blogging in her bedroom to editor-in-chief of her own online magazine and role model to millions of girls around the world.

It all started with Tavi's obsession with fashion. Even as a child, she loved expressing herself through her clothes, and would mix and match items she found at charity shops to create unique outfits. Sometimes her classmates would call her "weird" for her quirky style, but this only made Tavi more determined to stay true to herself.

In 2007, she learned that a friend's older sister had started a blog. Tavi had a passion for writing and fashion – maybe she could combine the two in her own blog? Within days she launched *Style Rookie*, which featured both her intelligent writing style and her passion for fashion. Pretty soon the blog was getting over 50,000 views a day, while the stylish schoolgirl was invited to attend top fashion shows and write articles for several leading fashion magazines.

The teenager was fast becoming a fashion force to be reckoned with. In 2009, she appeared on the cover of *Pop* magazine, while she was also asked to style several magazine photo shoots. But by age fifteen, Tavi already had a new mission in mind. After struggling to find strong female role models in her age group, she decided to create an online community where girls could come together to share their hopes, fears and dreams. That place was the online magazine *Rookie*, which Tavi launched in 2011 with the help of her mentors. *Rookie* is very different to the usual teen magazines. Not only is it written mainly by teenage girls for teenage girls, but it also focuses on the issues affecting them, such as body image and relationships, through articles such as "How to Not Care What People Think of You" and "As Brave as I Want to Be". Within five days of its launch, *Rookie* had received a million page views and was attracting followers from around the world.

Since then, Tavi has gone from strength to strength. In 2012, she took to the TEDxTeen stage to share her talk "A Teen Just Trying to Figure it Out". She has also branched out into film and theatre acting – at seventeen, she made her film debut in *Enough Said* while the following year she appeared on stage in *This is Our Youth*.

Today, Tavi is a successful entrepreneur in charge of a growing empire. But most important of all, she is proof that you should never be afraid to stand out from the crowd, because in doing so, you'll discover that you're not alone.

Fraser Doherty

1988– | JAM MAKER | SCOTLAND

If anyone knows the recipe for success, it's Fraser Doherty. At fourteen, his grandmother taught him how to make jam. Within a decade, SuperJam had transformed into a multi-million pound business and was named an "Iconic Scottish brand".

SuperJam is special because it's made from one-hundred-per-cent fruit with no added sugar or preservatives, making it a healthy alternative to other spreads. Soon, the jam was being sold at local fairs and farmers' markets, while Fraser was making a thousand jars a week in his parents' kitchen to keep up with the demand. Everything changed in 2007 when Fraser secured a deal to sell his produce through a leading UK supermarket chain, winning him millions of sales and several major awards.

Although Fraser's life is now jam-packed, he still finds time to give back to local communities by holding monthly "SuperJam Tea Parties" for elderly people living alone or in care homes.

Jordan Casey

2000– | APP DEVELOPER | IRELAND

When nine-year-old Jordan Casey persuaded his parents to buy him a computer, they thought he wanted it just to play video games. But Jordan was actually teaching himself to code with HTML. Soon the Irish schoolboy had created his first website, a fan blog for the game *Club Penguin*. By the age of twelve he'd launched his first game, *Alien Ball vs. Humans*, which shot straight to number one in Ireland's iTunes store.

From there, Jordan built more games and apps, and founded two companies – Casey Games and TeachWare, a cloud-based program that helps teachers to manage their students' exam and attendance records. Then, in 2016 Jordan launched *KidsCode*, a multiplayer virtual world that teaches children how to code through online games and puzzles.

Now, when he's not coding or doing his homework, Casey shares his passion for programming by speaking at tech events around the world.

Mabel Suglo

1993– | SHOEMAKER | GHANA

Mabel Suglo sees things differently. As a child, she saw how her grandmother suffered with leprosy, a contagious disease that causes painful sores and nerve damage. But although her granny struggled to find work due to her illness, she never gave up hope.

It was her grandmother's courage that inspired Mabel to help. While studying at the University for Developmental Studies in Ghana, Mabel raised enough money to start Eco-Shoes. The company provides disabled people with the training, skills and resources to make fashionable shoes and handbags from recycled fabric and car tyres. The employees have learned valuable skills and they now earn enough money to support themselves and their families.

In 2015, Mabel was runner-up in the Anzisha prize, Africa's main award for young entrepreneurs. True to form, she used the prize money to invest in more employees – because to her, business is all about helping others.

Mateusz Mach

1998– | APP DEVELOPER | POLAND

Polish teenager Mateusz Mach is a big fan of hip-hop. During high school, he designed an app that allowed him and his friends to send messages using rappers' hand signals.

But upon releasing the app in 2015, Mateusz was flooded with comments from deaf people thanking him for his creation, which for the first time allowed them to send texts in sign language. Realizing that he had stumbled upon a life-changing discovery, Mateusz asked for help from a team of coders, translators and investors. Within a year, *Five App*, the world's first messaging app using American Sign Language (ASL), was born. The app allows users to send more than 800 signs and even change the character's facial expression.

Mateusz's creation developed from a fun idea among friends to a whole new world of communication for millions of deaf people, proving that even the simplest inventions can go on to transform lives.

10 Ideas for Starting Your Own Business!

Do you have a cool idea for a new vlog channel? Perhaps you're a tech wizard? Or maybe you enjoy spending time with animals or young children? Whatever your passion, you can take your business idea all the way to the top! You'll also learn valuable skills, such as timekeeping, organization and responsibility along the way.

1

Start a YouTube channel or a blog based around your passion or hobby, such as fashion, sport, dancing or wildlife – whatever you like!

2

If you love animals, why not start a dog-walking or pet-sitting business with your friends?

3

If you enjoy taking photographs and editing them on your computer, why not offer your services to friends, family and neighbours?

6

If you love baking, why not sell your cupcake or cookie creations at the annual school fair?

7

If you're looking for a way to raise money for an upcoming event or holiday, ask your friends to help you set up and run a mobile car wash.

8

Are you a tech whizz? You could offer your services to friends and neighbours. Or start your own website or YouTube channel, including how-to videos that show how to fix basic tech problems.

Before attempting any of the following ideas, make sure to ask for your parents' permission. If you're under fourteen, you should also ask your parents, another family member or your teacher to help you with setting up your business and to accompany you where necessary.

Staying safe on the internet!

The internet and social media are great tools for starting a business. But sometimes information posted online can get into the wrong hands. To make sure you stay safe when using the internet, always stick to the following rules:

Never give out your personal information to strangers online. This includes your name, your telephone number, and your home and email address.

Instead of using your real name as a user name, why not come up with a fun, memorable nickname instead? Not only will this make your business more recognizable but you'll also protect your real-life identity.

Always get your parents' permission before posting anything, including photos and videos, to the internet.

Always check with your parents before downloading anything from the internet or joining any new websites.

4

Busy parents always need babysitters. If you're responsible and good with younger children, you could offer your services to neighbours and family friends.

5

Do you have a talent for crafts? With your parents' help, you could sell your homemade jewellery or greeting cards at a local shop or through a craft website.

9

Do you like to draw logos and other fun designs? With your parents' help, you could put your designs on T-shirts and sell them online, or to family and friends.

10

You don't always have to make money through your business. How about setting up a used clothes and toy stall at your school fair, and donating the money you raise to a local charity?

Mark Zuckerberg

1984– | FOUNDER OF FACEBOOK | USA

You've probably already heard of Mark Zuckerberg, Facebook's creator and one of the world's richest people. But did you know that Mark was at middle school when he first started programming and writing software?

At twelve, Mark used Atari BASIC software to develop his first games and programs. These included "ZuckNet", a messaging system that connected all the computers in his home. Then, during high school he built the Synapse media player, one of the first music programs to remember the listener's music tastes and make suggestions for playlists. Within a month of its release, Synapse was downloaded over 10,000 times! This led to Mark receiving several job offers from major tech companies, including Microsoft, but instead he decided to apply to Harvard University to study computer science and psychology. In hindsight this was the right choice, because it was there that Mark created the website that would change his life.

In his second year, Mark began developing a program to connect students across Harvard. By 4th February 2004, the "Facebook" was ready for launch. Within hours, around 1,500 Harvard students had registered. By March, half of all Harvard students were using the site and Mark released it to other universities around the USA. Cut to 2012 and Facebook had gone public, attracting a billion users worldwide! That same year, *Vanity Fair* magazine named Mark Most Influential Person of the Information Age.

Today, Mark is still chairman and CEO of Facebook and is estimated to be worth around $70.9 billion. But he uses his fortune for good. In 2010, he signed The Giving Pledge, a campaign that encourages the world's richest people to donate huge amounts of their money to charities and scientific research.

His journey from programming prodigy to Facebook founder and philanthropist has made Mark one of history's most successful entrepreneurs and an inspiration to millions.

ARTS AND LITERATURE

Do you love drawing or painting pictures of your favourite people, places or animals? Perhaps you're always coming up with ideas for stories set in imaginary worlds? Maybe you enjoy taking photographs or writing poetry, and sharing your creations with friends and family? If so, then congratulations – you've taken your first steps to becoming an artist!

Art is important to everyone. Not only does it allow us to express our thoughts and feelings, our hopes and fears, but it also brings us joy or helps us to relax when we're having a bad day or going through a difficult time. When we curl up with a good book or visit an art gallery we're transported to another world, where we can let our imaginations run wild. Often good art helps us to make sense of the world or connects us to other cultures. It moves us, inspires us and excites us.

And if there's another truly amazing thing about art, it's that anyone can get involved at any age! Christopher Paolini and Beth Reekles wrote best-selling novels in their teens. Misty Copeland was an award-winning ballet dancer by fifteen. Hamzah Marbella, Kieron Williamson and Wang Yani had created hundreds of masterpieces before they'd finished primary school. David Uzochukwu and Jay Hulme had produced award-winning art before reaching adulthood, while Nina Lugovskaya wrote her best-selling diary while she was still a schoolgirl.

Today, the internet and social media have made it even simpler for budding artists to share their creations. By uploading a story or photo to the web, you can reach a possible audience of thousands in an instant. With so much to inspire you and so little to stop you, maybe it's time to unleash your own creativity on the world.

Misty Copeland

Misty Copeland is a shining star. As a child she hadn't even heard of ballet. She didn't take part in her first dance class until she was thirteen. But twenty years later, Misty made history when she became the first-ever African-American female principal dancer at the American Ballet Theatre (ABT), one of the USA's leading classical ballet companies.

Misty was born in Kansas City, Missouri. Her parents divorced when she was two and she, her mum and her five siblings moved to California. Things were tough: the entire family lived in a single motel room and Misty's mum had to work several jobs to feed them. Misty also lacked confidence and was extremely shy. But when she began attending the local Boys

"You can start late, look different, be uncertain and still succeed."

& Girls Club (an organization that provides after-school activities for young people), her life changed forever.

There, Misty took part in a free dance class and revealed a surprising natural talent. Ballet teacher Cindy Bradley was so impressed by the teenager's grace and ability to remember difficult steps that she asked her to train at her private school, the San Pedro Dance Center. Within days of arriving, Misty had found a passion for ballet and a mentor in Cindy to guide her.

Most dancers start training as toddlers. At thirteen, Misty was a late starter, but that only made her more determined. After three months she was dancing en pointe (on the tips of the toes). By fifteen, she had won her first solo role and placed first at the Los Angeles Music Center Spotlight Awards!

Next, Misty won a scholarship to the San Francisco Ballet School's summer workshop. She had a lot of catching up to do, and she struggled with the fact that she was the only African-American girl in her class, but by the end of the workshop the school offered her a full-time place. However, the young dancer had another ballet company in her sights…

Ballet dancers are known for their grace and elegance as they effortlessly glide across the stage. But behind the scenes, ballet is an extremely gruelling art form. Professionals must train and rehearse for around ten hours a day, six days a week, and follow a strict diet and fitness routine. Injuries are common, and Misty herself has battled several that threatened to end her career.

But the hard work finally paid off – in 2000, Misty was selected to join her dream company, the ABT in New York City. In 2007, she was promoted to soloist and performed the leads in *Don Quixote*, *Sleeping Beauty* and *The Firebird* to rave reviews. Finally, she was promoted to principal dancer in 2015, the crowning achievement in an already sparkling career.

Since then Misty has continued to leave a lasting impression – in 2015 *Time* magazine named her one of the 100 most influential people in the world. At 5ft 2in, Misty may be small, but she is a giant of the stage and a role model to all those striving to make their dreams come true, no matter their background.

Christopher Paolini

1983– | AUTHOR | USA

As a child, Christopher Paolini loved reading the fantasy novels of J.R.R. Tolkien and Philip Pullman – so much so that by sixteen, he'd written his own! Christopher began work on *Eragon*, the first book in the *Inheritance Cycle* series, upon finishing high school. The story centres on Eragon, a farmboy who finds a strange stone in the mountains. But then the "stone", which is really an egg, begins to crack … revealing a baby dragon.

Christopher spent two years writing the book before self-publishing in 2002 with his parents' help. By chance, author Carl Hiaasen discovered *Eragon* in a bookshop and was so impressed with it, he took it to a major publisher, who rereleased the book in 2003. Eragon topped several bestseller lists while the series, which also includes *Eldest*, *Brisingr* and *Inheritance*, has since sold 35 million worldwide.

Next up for Christopher is another potential bestseller – his first science fiction novel!

Nina Lugovskaya

1918–1993 | DIARIST | RUSSIA

Nina Lugovskaya grew up in the Soviet Union (in Russia) during Joseph Stalin's rule. At thirteen, she started to keep a diary. It contained her hopes and dreams, including her ambition to become a writer.

In 1935, Nina's father was arrested and exiled from Moscow for opposing Stalin's rule. The teenager recorded her feelings about the arrest in her diary. But in 1937, the Soviet secret police force searched the family's apartment and seized the diary. Nina, her mother and sisters were arrested for treason and sentenced to five years' hard labour in a gulag (labour camp). The women survived, but they were exiled to Siberia upon their release.

After Nina died in 1993, a historian discovered her diary in the Soviet records. *The Diary of a Soviet Schoolgirl* was finally published in 2003 and became a bestseller.

David Uzochukwu

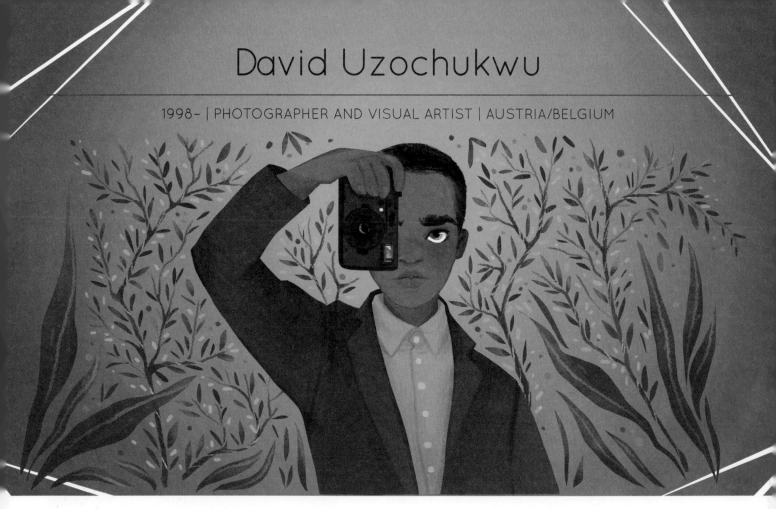

When photographer David Uzochukwu was just eighteen, the British singer-songwriter FKA Twigs selected him to shoot an advertising campaign she was working on with Nike. Since then, his photography and self-portraits have featured in magazines and on billboards around the world.

David's family is originally from Nigeria. He was born in Austria, and his family moved to Luxembourg when he was six. He first picked up a camera at the age of ten while on holiday, and from that moment on he was hooked. David was inspired by Luxembourg's landscapes and began taking photos of his surroundings. When he signed up to Flickr to share his images online, he discovered a group of young artists and photographers who encouraged him to develop his craft. Soon, he was spending his spare time trawling hundreds of online tutorials and developing his unique style. By thirteen he was experimenting with self-portraits and producing dreamy and bold landscape photos.

Before long, David's work had caught the attention of the art world. At sixteen, he was asked to shoot several top magazine and advertising projects. In 2014, he was named the EyeEm Photographer of the Year, while the following year he was one of twenty-five visual artists selected to produce a new image to celebrate Adobe Photoshop's twenty-fifth anniversary.

Since then, David, who now lives in Belgium, has built up an impressive collection of images. His work has been published in top magazines like *Vogue* and *Wonderland*, and on the fashion website Refinery29, while David has gained thousands of fans through social media. With so much success at the start of his career, the future looks bright for this young photographer.

> "I want to be creating work that actually aims to change something; that challenges the viewer and is not simply easy on the eyes."

Hamzah Marbella

2001– | ARTIST | PHILLIPINES

By the time Hamzah Marbella was nine, he had already produced an incredible 300 paintings. Around fifty of these were award-winning works, while some have even been displayed at the United Nations headquarters in New York City.

It helps that Hamzah has parents who support him every step of the way. But growing up in the Philippines, surrounded by tropical landscapes, wildlife and flowers, is another bonus, because Hamzah's vibrant surroundings are the inspiration behind his bold and colourful paintings. Many of his pieces also feature glowing suns and his favourite animals – fish and cats.

Now Hamzah's art is capturing hearts around the world. Not only has he exhibited his work in several other countries, but his painting *Bounty* also sold for around £6,000 at a professional art auction! No wonder this talented teen is inspiring thousands of children to pick up their paintbrushes.

Beth Reekles

1995– | AUTHOR | UK

Fifteen-year-old Beth Reeks was tired of reading the same old stories for teens, featuring wizards, werewolves and vampires, so she decided to do something about it. While studying for her GCSEs she wrote *The Kissing Booth*, a young-adult novel about normal kids dealing with normal relationships. Beth uploaded it to the story-sharing website Wattpad under her pen name, Beth Reekles. She thought it would be a fun creative outlet but the story soon had an incredible 19 million views.

Due to her online success, in 2012 Beth won a contract to publish her first book, plus two more novels, *The Rolling Dice* and *Out of Tune*. *The Kissing Booth* has since been made into a movie, while in 2013 *Time* magazine named Beth as one of the world's most influential teenagers. Her stories may be down to earth, but this is one young author who has reached for the stars!

Kieron Williamson

2002– | ARTIST | UK

It often takes years for an artist to master his craft, but not so for Kieron Williamson, who already had an international following by age six. Since then, Kieron's paintings have earned him an amazing £2 million, while this "mini Monet" has been compared to some of the most influential artists in history.

Kieron was born and raised in Holt, a small town in Norfolk. But it was on a family holiday to Cornwall that he first discovered his passion for art. The five-year-old was so inspired by the Cornish coast with its pretty boats and harbours that he asked his parents for some proper paper and paints. Within days, he had produced a handful of paintings that revealed a surprising talent.

Back at home, Kieron's parents – neither of whom is artistic – enrolled him in several local art classes and workshops. There he learned some of the more practical aspects of painting.

However, he was already developing his own style, inspired by the wide-open skies and rolling rivers and marshes of Norfolk, and his favourite landscape artist, Norfolk-born Edward Seago.

Before long, his watercolours had captured the attention of the local Holt art gallery, which exhibited his work for the first time when Kieron was just six. Word of Kieron's talent soon spread, and during his second exhibition, all sixteen paintings sold out in just fourteen minutes. At his next show, everything sold out within thirty minutes, for a total of £150,000!

Today there is a long waiting list for Kieron's masterpieces, while he has progressed from watercolours to using acrylics, pastels and oils. Yet, while it's nice being known as a world-class artist, nothing makes Kieron happier than standing at his easel, capturing the landscapes of his beloved Norfolk on canvas.

Arts and Literature Prodigies Through History

Throughout history, children and teens have created influential and celebrated works of art and literature. From one of the largest paintings in Chinese history to the best-selling diary of all time, these young storytellers, artists and poets made masterpieces that stood the test of time.

1113 The Chinese painter **Wang Ximeng** (1096–1119) was eighteen when he finished *A Thousand Li of Rivers and Mountains*. At 11.9m (39ft) long, it is one of China's largest-ever paintings.

1804 The American poet and journalist **William Cullen Bryant** (1794–1878) was just ten when his first works were published in the *North American Review*, the USA's first literary magazine. He went on to become one of the USA's most celebrated poets and editor of the *New York Evening Post*.

1840 The English painter and illustrator **John Everett Millais** (1829–1896) attended the Royal Academy of Arts from age eleven, making him the school's youngest-ever student. He co-founded the Pre-Raphaelite Brotherhood, an art movement that included William Morris and Dante Gabriel Rossetti.

1869 Bangladesh's **Rabindranath Tagore** (1861–1941) was famous for his poetry, plays, novels, short stories, paintings and songs. He wrote his first poem in 1869, at eight, and by sixteen he had published his first poetry. He completed thousands of works over his lifetime, including eight novels, hundreds of short stories and more than 2,000 songs. In 1913, he won the Nobel Prize in Literature for his poetry collection *Gitanjali*.

1889 The painter, sculptor and illustrator **Pablo Picasso** (1881–1973) is regarded as the most influential artist of the twentieth century. He was nine when he completed his first major painting, *Picador*, and was admitted to Barcelona's School of Fine Arts at just thirteen. He is best known for co-founding the Cubist movement. Cubism is an influential art form that depicts everyday objects as their basic geometrical shapes. Pablo's most famous painting – 1937's *Guernica*, which shows the bombing of Guernica during the Spanish Civil War – is a world-famous example of the Cubist style.

1927 The American writer **Barbara Newhall Follett** (1914–1939) published her first novel, *The House Without Windows*, when she was twelve, followed by her second, *The Voyage of the Norman D.*, at age fourteen.

1945 Anne Frank (1929–1945) was a Jewish girl growing up in the Netherlands. During the Second World War, she and her family were forced to hide from the Nazis in a secret annex. To occupy herself, Anne kept a diary. But after two years, the Nazis discovered the group's hiding place and deported them to the concentration camps. Anne escaped the gas chambers but she died from disease at fifteen, only a few weeks before the Allies freed her camp. Her father survived and upon discovering Anne's diary in the annex, he had it published in 1947. *The Diary of Anne Frank* became one of the best-selling books of all time.

1967 The American writer **S.E. (Susan) Hinton** (1948–) wrote her first novel, *The Outsiders*, while still at high school. The novel, set in Oklahoma, USA, was inspired by rival gangs the Greasers and the Socs, at Susan's school. It eventually sold over 14 million copies.

1981 Indian artist **Edmund Thomas Clint** (1976–1983) began drawing before he was one and in 1981, at age five, he won a prestigious competition for under-18 painters. In all, he painted over 30,000 pieces before tragically dying from kidney failure aged six years and eleven months.

1993 The American poet **Mattie Stepanek** (1990–2004) started writing poetry at just three. He went on to publish six volumes of poetry and a collection of essays, before dying from a rare cell disease at thirteen.

1998 The Australian writer, artist and now comedian **Ash Lieb** (1982–) held his first art exhibit at eight and wrote his first novel, *The Secret Well* (1998), at fifteen.

2008 The American photographer and filmmaker **Alex Currie** (1998–) shot his first photos and films in 2008, aged ten. He also shot the cover for the band NF's album *Therapy Session* and directed several music videos before he turned eighteen.

Wang Yani

1975– | ARTIST | CHINA

Wang Yani began painting at just two and a half years old. By four, she'd had her first exhibition in Shanghai. When she was eight, one of her pieces appeared on a Chinese postage stamp!

Wang's father was also an artist, but he gave up his career to help his daughter develop her style. He taught her Chinese brush painting, a traditional technique that uses the "Four Treasures": brush, rice paper, ink stone and ink stick. When her father bought her a pet monkey, Wang painted the animal in mischievous poses among water buffalos, trees and flowers.

Soon Wang had created thousands of pieces and grew from a national treasure to a global star. At sixteen, she also became the youngest artist ever to have a solo show at the Smithsonian Institution in Washington, DC.

Jay Hulme

1997– | PERFORMANCE POET | UK

Jay Hulme believes that performance poetry is so powerful because it allows performers to speak openly and honestly about the challenges they face. This is especially important to him, since many of his poems draw on his personal life, particularly his experiences of growing up transgender.

By seventeen, Jay had already made a name for himself on the UK art scene. In 2015 he won SLAMbassadors UK, the country's biggest competition for young performance poets. That same year he published his first collection of poems, *The Prospect of Wings*, followed by his second, *City Boys Should Not Feed Horses*, in 2016.

Jay believes that poetry belongs to everyone. As such, he now holds workshops at schools, libraries and festivals around the UK, inspiring thousands of young people to fall in love with his favourite art form.

POLITICS AND ACTIVISM

What does the word "politics" mean to you? Do you picture famous world leaders giving historic speeches? Perhaps you think of iconic government buildings, like the Houses of Parliament in the UK or the Capitol Building in the USA. Maybe you're familiar with some of the big issues affecting the planet, such as war, poverty and human rights. All of these things can make it seem like politics has very little to do with ordinary people. But in fact, no matter where you live, no matter how old you are, politics affects all of us, every day.

Governments create the laws that govern our society. They help to determine how schools, hospitals and the emergency services run, and how much we pay in taxes to preserve these resources. And for those who live in a democracy, once you're old enough, you'll get the chance to vote in elections to choose the leaders of your country.

But as the children in this section prove, you don't have to wait until you're an adult to get involved in politics, nor do you have to be a politician! Sophie Scholl bravely fought injustice during a turbulent time in her country. Jazz Jennings, Malala Yousafzai, Payal Jangid and Nkosi Johnson have campaigned for change within their communities. Mhairi Black and Brandon Green represent young people on the political stage, while Dylan Mahalingham and Jeremy Heimans have organized youth participation on a global scale.

No matter their goal, these children have one thing in common – through passion and belief, they are helping to create a brighter future for all.

Sophie Scholl

1921–1943 | POLITICAL ACTIVIST | GERMANY

"What does my death matter, if through us, thousands of people are awakened and stirred to action?"

In 1933, when Adolf Hitler came to power in Germany, life for many citizens changed overnight. Hitler viewed Jews as enemies of the state and restricted their freedoms. With the passing of the Nuremberg Laws in 1935, Jews were stripped of their citizenship, forbidden from marrying non-Jews and eventually banned from public places, such as swimming pools, cinemas and certain schools and workplaces.

Sophie Scholl was born in Forchtenberg in 1921. As Lutheran Christians, the Scholl family believed that every person had the right to a dignified life. Even though the Nuremberg Laws didn't directly affect her, Sophie found them troubling. When two Jewish friends were barred from joining her in the League of German Girls, Sophie found it harder to ignore her conscience. Then, in 1937 the police arrested her brother, Hans, for speaking out, while her father was later sent to prison for criticizing the government.

In 1942, Sophie enrolled at Munich University and surrounded herself with friends who shared her beliefs. That year Hans started the White Rose, a group that criticized the war and promoted freedom of speech. The group worked in total secret, producing six anti-war leaflets and circulating them anonymously. Sophie joined when she realized that because she was a girl, the police were less likely to search her.

But on 18th February 1943, Sophie's luck ran out. She was caught distributing leaflets in the university library and was arrested. After a short trial, she and several other White Rose members, including Hans, were sentenced to death. Sophie was just twenty-one.

Today, the group are honoured as heroes in Germany. Many streets, squares and schools are named after Sophie and Hans, while in 2003 the government of Bavaria placed a statue of Sophie in Walhalla, a memorial building that honours the most distinguished people in German history.

Nkosi Johnson

1989–2001 | AIDS ACTIVIST | SOUTH AFRICA

Around 7 million South Africans currently live with HIV/AIDS, while each year thousands of children, like Nkosi Johnson, are born HIV-positive.

Gail Johnson adopted Nkosi when his mother became too ill to care for him. But when she tried to enrol him at a local primary school, the school refused to accept him, due to his illness. The story made national news, since it is illegal in South Africa to segregate people on medical grounds. However, Nkosi saw the event as his chance to help fellow AIDS sufferers.

In 1999, Nkosi and Gail opened Nkosi's Haven, a centre that provides support and shelter to mothers and children with AIDS. In 2000, Nkosi delivered an inspirational speech at the 13th International AIDS Conference.

Sadly, Nkosi succumbed to AIDS at twelve. Four years later, and in honour of the courage he'd demonstrated throughout his short life, he was awarded the first International Children's Peace Prize.

Jazz Jennings

2000– | LGBTQ ACTIVIST | USA

Jazz Jennings is like any other teenage girl, except that she has already faced more challenges in her life than many ever will, being transgender. Although Jazz's family have always supported her, they worried she would struggle to find acceptance. But Jazz didn't want to hide her true self. Instead, she decided to speak out and use her experience for good.

In 2007, she and her parents founded the TransKids Purple Rainbow Foundation to provide both emotional and financial support to trans youth. Jazz has also brought change to her community: when she was prevented from playing for the local girls' football team, she and her parents fought – and won – a long court battle to change the rules, giving trans students the right to play.

Since then, Jazz has continued to share her message of love and tolerance, making her a hero to children around the world.

Dylan Mahalingam

1995– | FOUNDER OF LIL' MDGS | USA

When Dylan Mahalingam travelled to India with his family, he was shocked to see extreme poverty for the first time. But instead of feeling powerless to help, Dylan was inspired to act.

When he heard about the United Nations' Millennium Development Goals (MDGs), he saw his opportunity. With the support of their parents, nine-year-old Dylan and his cousins formed Lil' MDGs. The organization encourages children around the world to get involved in meeting the targets of the eight MDGs.

So what exactly are the MDGs? At the Millennium Summit in 2000, more than a hundred United Nations member states made a commitment to reduce global poverty and make the world a better, safer place for all by 2015. They created eight goals to help them achieve their target:

1. Reduce poverty and extreme hunger.
2. Educate every primary school-age child.
3. Provide equal opportunities for women and girls.
4. Reduce the number of infant deaths.
5. Improve the health of women during pregnancy.
6. Combat HIV/AIDS, malaria and other infectious diseases.
7. Improve environmental sustainability (by reducing pollution and the destruction of natural resources).
8. Make the world a better place by sharing new technologies and providing access to better medicine in developing countries.

Through these goals, the UN hoped to lift 500 million people out of poverty within fifteen years. If the MDGs hit their target, they would improve the lives of millions around the world:

people would receive medicine to treat disease, fewer infants would die and more children would attend school.

Lil' MDGs has since gone on to engage more than 3 million children in forty-seven countries around the world in its mission. The organization provides its volunteers with the resources and tools to set up fundraisers and get help from local businesses to promote their events. The funds have been used in hundreds of projects, from providing a mobile hospital for treating villagers in India to building a playground for orphans in Uganda. Lil' MDGs also raised $780,000 for the victims of the 2004 earthquake and tsunami in South East Asia and $10 million to help people rebuild their homes after hurricanes Katrina and Rita in the USA.

From natural disasters to AIDS awareness, the Lil' MDGs volunteers have been there every step of the way.

The 2015 deadline for the MDGs has now passed and the United Nations has replaced them with seventeen new Sustainable Development Goals, which aim to continue the work of the previous goals. Since then, Dylan has gone on to become a United Nations youth speaker. Not only does he speak at UN summits around the world, but he also runs workshops in schools and around the local community. Everywhere he goes, Dylan has one message – no matter how far apart they are, when children come together, they can make a world of difference.

"Our mission is to educate, engage, inspire, and empower children in all corners of the world to work together to forward the UN Millennium Development Goals."

Payal Jangid

2002– | CHILDREN'S RIGHTS ACTIVIST | INDIA

Jeremy Heimans

1978– | DIGITAL ACTIVIST | AUSTRALIA

Payal Jangid was born in Hinsala, a rural village in Rajasthan state, India. There, many girls were dropping out of school to start work at a young age. But Payal was determined to secure a better education for the girls of her village.

Her chance finally came through Child-Friendly Villages, a nonprofit organization that believes every child has the right to an education. When members of the organization arrived in Hinsala, they helped to set up a Children's Parliament. Eleven-year-old Payal was elected as its chief, and ever since she has campaigned tirelessly to encourage every child in Hinsala to enrol in school.

In 2013, Payal was also selected as a jury member of the World Children's Prize, an organization that gives children a chance to engage in positive change. Today Payal travels all over the world as she continues her inspirational campaign.

Since the age of eight, Jeremy Heimans has been on a mission to change the world. At first he thought he needed to become a politician to make a difference, but he soon realized that big government institutions can make change slow and difficult.

That was when Jeremy turned to technology. First, he sent messages to global leaders through a fax machine. Then, as technology developed, Jeremy used the power of the internet and social media to encourage millions of young people to get involved in political decision-making.

Since then, Jeremy has founded several of the world's largest online political movements, including GetUp!, Avaaz and Purpose. Through these organizations, he provides tools and resources to help young people engage with issues like climate change and poverty. He is proof that when ordinary people work together, they can make an extraordinary difference.

Brandon Green

2001– | MEMBER OF THE UK YOUTH PARLIAMENT | UK

On 10th November 2017, sixteen-year-old Brandon Green was given a once-in-a-lifetime opportunity. As a member of the UK Youth Parliament (UKYP), representing Yorkshire and Humber, he was selected as one of five debate leads (a person who gives a speech to introduce a topic for debate) at the UKYP's Annual Sitting in the House of Commons. On a normal day in the Commons, members of parliament (MPs) propose new laws and vote on government policies, such as those affecting the economy, education and healthcare. But during the Annual Sitting, MPs make way for over 200 UKYP members, who come together to debate the issues that affect young people every day.

The UKYP is an elected body that gives young people the opportunity to influence how the country is run. Children from across the UK are elected in yearly elections, and anyone between the ages of eleven and eighteen – including you!

– can stand or vote. Once elected, members run campaigns, organize events and attend historic debates, like the Annual Sitting.

The UKYP also gives millions of young people a chance to have their say. Each year, children vote to select the topics for the UKYP's national campaign. In 2017, those topics included work experience, a "curriculum for life" and lowering the voting age for general elections, from eighteen to sixteen. With all eyes on him, Brandon proudly stood up in the Commons and introduced the debate on improving public transport.

While studying for his A levels at Barnsley sixth-form college, Brandon is also working with the Barnsley Youth Council. He is helping to make real changes in his community and showing young people that they really can achieve anything they set their minds to.

Young Leaders Through History

You may think it impossible for a child to rule a nation, but there is actually a long list of young leaders throughout history. Most mini monarchs are next in line to the throne, meaning that when their parent – a king, queen or emperor – dies, they are thrust into leadership at an early age. But nobody expects a youngster to lead a country. They usually have powerful advisers who run things for them until the true heir is old enough to govern his or her country and its people.

1332 BC The Egyptian pharaoh **Tutankhamen** (c.1341–c.1323 BC) was just nine or ten years old when he ascended to the throne. He eventually became known as the "boy king".

c.51 BC The Egyptian ruler **Ptolemy XIII** (c.62/61–47 BC) came to power at age eleven or twelve. He married his older sister, Cleopatra, but when her power as queen grew, a war broke out between the two and their supporters. Ptolemy apparently drowned in the River Nile in 47 BC while attempting to escape from soldiers, leaving Cleopatra to take the throne.

AD 309 **Shapur II the Great** (309–379) was the tenth king of the Sasanian Empire, which covered much of the modern-day Middle East. According to one legend, he was crowned before he was born! Shapur II is also the longest-reigning monarch in Iran's history, as he ruled for seventy years, from before his birth right up to his death in AD 379.

AD 218

The Roman emperor **Elagabalus** (c.203–222) came to power at age fifteen. He reigned for four years, during which he supposedly married five times! His leadership was so unpopular that his grandmother devised a plot to have him assassinated, when he was eighteen. He was replaced by his cousin, Severus Alexander.

1542 **Mary, Queen of Scots** (1542–1587) inherited the crown when her father, King James V, died. She was just six days old! She was far too young to rule, and spent most of her childhood in France while regents governed Scotland. Mary was a Catholic, and Scotland's leading Protestants contested her rule, leading to violent uprisings. In 1561, she returned to Scotland, only to be kidnapped and imprisoned several times. She finally faced trial over a plot to kill Elizabeth I, Queen of England. Mary denied the charges but she was found guilty and executed on 8th February 1587.

1623 Murad IV (1612–1640) was eleven when he became sultan of the Ottoman Empire. His mother, Kösem Sultan, ruled over the empire before Murad was old enough to reign.

1632 Queen Christina of Sweden (1626–1689) ascended to the throne at age six, when her father died in battle, but turned eighteen before she began to rule alone. Christina was a modern woman for the time: she often wore men's clothes, was highly educated, loved to read books and was a supporter of the arts. She never married, and abdicated the throne in 1654 to her cousin, Charles Gustav. Christina remained active in politics until her death from pneumonia in 1689.

1643 Louis XIV of France (1638–1715) began his reign at age five, although he wasn't formally crowned until 1654, at fifteen. Before then, a regent council ruled over France on Louis' behalf. Louis was a popular ruler, and he became known as Louis the Great. But he suffered from many illnesses, including diabetes and boils. He died in 1715 after seventy-two years on the throne, making him the longest-reigning monarch in Europe's history.

1643 Five-year-old Fulin (1638–1661) was the third emperor of China's Qing Dynasty and the first person to rule over China as a whole. His uncle Dorgon ruled as regent for the first few years of Fulin's life. When Dorgon died in 1650, Fulin ruled until his death from smallpox at twenty-two.

1886 Spain's Alfonso XIII (1886–1941) became king upon birth, as his father died before he was born. However, he didn't assume power until 1902, at the age of sixteen.

1995 Rukirabasaija Oyo Nyimba Kabamba Iguru Rukidi IV (1992–), known as King Oyo, became leader of the Toro Kingdom in Uganda at age three when his father died. Uganda has several such kingdoms with their own monarchs, but these kingdoms are no longer sovereign – rather, the country is governed by a president, while the kingdoms' monarchs serve mainly as cultural figures.

Malala Yousafzai

1997– | EDUCATION ACTIVIST | PAKISTAN

Malala Yousafzai was an ordinary schoolgirl who became a leading education activist. When an armed group took control of her hometown in Swat District, Pakistan, they stopped girls attending school. But Malala was an excellent student. She believed in her right to an education, and she made it her mission to speak out.

However, when the fifteen-year-old was travelling home from school one day, a gunman boarded the bus and shot her. Malala was lucky to survive, and she received get-well cards from children around the world. After her recovery she was invited to speak at the United Nations on her sixteenth birthday. Then, in 2014, she became the youngest person ever to win the Nobel Peace Prize. Three years later, she also became the youngest United Nations Messenger of Peace in history.

Mhairi Black

1994– | POLITICIAN | SCOTLAND, UK

Mhairi Black is famous for breaking barriers. In 2015, at the age of twenty years and 237 days, she was elected MP for Paisley and Renfrewshire South, making her the youngest person since 1880 to serve in the UK parliament. She is also not afraid to stand up for what she believes in. As a representative of the Scottish National Party, in July 2015 she made a speech to Parliament that criticized the government for not doing enough to protect poorer people in Scotland. Within days, the passionate speech went viral and Mhairi became a figurehead for the people who shared her views.

Since becoming Britain's youngest MP, Mhairi has spoken of her desire to see poor and young people have a brighter future. And after winning her seat for a second time, in the 2017 general election, Mhairi has at least another four years to make her goals a reality.

THE FUTURE IS IN YOUR HANDS!

This book celebrates the amazing children who are transforming the world before they even reach adulthood. Through passion, determination and a desire to help others, they are solving environmental problems, making incredible discoveries and entertaining millions. From the talented trailblazers who have already made their mark, to the inventors, entrepreneurs and superstars of the future, these children are proof that you are never too young to make the world a better place.

You may think it an impossible task to follow in their footsteps. But however talented they are, all of these children have had to work hard. Many faced obstacles to success, yet they persevered and prevailed against the odds. Some came from poor backgrounds or difficult circumstances but their curiosity took them to places they never thought possible.

Most are just ordinary kids with extraordinary imaginations, while others discovered their passion by accident. Whether you're a tech whizz or a talented singer, are drawn to caring for others, animals and the environment, or you're passionate about standing up for your beliefs, there is already a young hero to show you the way.

So, could you be the next Richard Turere or Taylor Swift? Maybe you aspire to the success of Lydia Ko or Christopher Paolini? Perhaps you dream of making a big difference, like Boyan Slat or Marita Cheng? Whatever your goal in life, and however you choose to get there, these children's stories teach us one simple lesson: the future is in your hands! Because you never know … one day, it could be your turn to inspire the next generation of young heroes.

Ways to be a Hero Every Day

The children in this book have achieved so many great things. But you don't have to climb Mount Everest or write a best-selling novel to join them: you'll find life can be just as rewarding if every day you are kind, helpful and respectful to those around you.

At home

* BE KIND By spreading kindness, you can help to make your home a happier place.

* BE HELPFUL Offer to lend a hand with chores around the house. Your parents will be glad of the help and you'll also learn new skills and responsibilities along the way.

* BE HONEST Sometimes we can make the wrong decisions, but it's best to own up to your mistakes rather than hide them. This will help you to grow as a person and to build a trusting relationship with your family.

* BE THOUGHTFUL Send a thank-you card or email to someone when they show you kindness or bring you a gift. Give them a gift or a card when they're ill or feeling down.

* BE CARING If one of your family members is having a hard day, show them that you care by offering help or finding a way to cheer them up.

At school

* WORK HARD By focusing in lessons and completing your work on time, you'll show respect to your teachers, your fellow classmates and yourself.

* BE FAIR Everyone has feelings. No matter their background, treat all of your classmates just as you'd like to be treated – with respect and kindness.

* SPEAK UP Be a good friend. If you see someone being bullied at school, tell a teacher or your parents.

* BE A GOOD ROLE MODEL Always set a good example to your classmates and the younger children in school. It feels nice to have someone look up to you!

* PRACTISE SHARING Learning to share takes practice but the more you do it, the more friends you'll gain.

* GET INVOLVED Share your talents! Take part in after-school clubs, school plays and sports teams.

There are so many ways to be amazing every day, whether you're at home, at school, out in your community or in the wider world. By learning these valuable life skills now, not only will you become a better citizen, but you'll also be on the right path to achieving your dreams.

In your community

- VOLUNTEER Volunteering is a great way to help others less fortunate than you, while you'll make friends and learn new skills along the way. You could help at an animal shelter or organize a litter pick in your local park.

- BE POLITE Don't forget to say "please" and "thank you" to everyone who has a positive impact on your day, from the school bus driver to your dinner lady.

- OBEY LAWS Laws are put into place to protect communities, the people that live in them and their property. Always remember to set a good example by following them.

- PROTECT THE COMMUNITY Help keep your community clean by picking up litter and avoiding damage to other people's property.

- SPEAK OUT Just because you're young, that doesn't mean you can't have a voice. If you're passionate about a certain issue and want to make a difference, ask your parents to help you contact your local government representatives.

In the wider world

- BE A GOOD CITIZEN There are lots of ways to raise funds for charities that help people in need, from organizing a bake sale to a sponsored swim.

- TAKE TRIPS Whether you're visiting your local zoo, another city or a far-flung country, going on a trip is a great opportunity to learn new things and experience other cultures.

- PROTECT THE ENVIRONMENT Remember the three Rs – reduce, reuse and recycle!

- BE POSITIVE The world is changing every day and it can sometimes feel overwhelming. But remember to stay positive and spread happiness.

- NEVER GIVE UP Life can be tough, but it is important to stay strong so that you can overcome challenges. And remember – never be afraid to ask for help or offer it to others in need.

More Young Heroes

Age 1

Tiger Woods, Golfer, USA (1975): Started playing golf. Went on to become one of the most successful golfers and sportsmen of all time.

Age 2

Tristan Pang, Mathematician and Scientist, UK/New Zealand (2001–): Started high school maths and learned to read independently. Delivered a TED Talk at age eleven, becoming one of the youngest speakers in the world.

Wayne Gretzky, Ice Hockey Player, Canada (1961–): Started playing ice hockey. Became one of the greatest pro hockey players ever and is nicknamed "The Great One".

Age 3

Aman Rehman, Digital Animator, India (2001–): Created his first digital computer animation, Dancing Alphabets. Began teaching animation at thirteen, becoming the world's youngest lecturer.

Age 3

Onafujiri Remet, Photographer, Nigeria (2010–): Held his first photography exhibition, in Lagos, Nigeria's largest city.

Age 4

Julian Bliss, Clarinettist, UK (1989–): Started playing clarinet. Performed at Queen Elizabeth II's Golden Jubilee at age thirteen.

Age 5

Alisa Sadikova, Harpist, Russia (2003–): Started playing the harp. Has since performed with top orchestras around the world.

Age 6

Mickey Rooney, Actor, USA (1920–2014): Appeared in his first film *Not to be Trusted*. Acted in more than 300 films over the next nine decades.

Age 7

Akrit Jaswal, India (1993–): The medical genius became known as "the youngest surgeon in the world" when he performed his first successful operation on a young burn victim's hand. At twelve, Jawal became India's youngest-ever university student when he was admitted to Punjab University to study for a bachelors in science. He has since earned a masters degree and is now focused on developing a cure for cancer.

Age 8

Alexandra Nechita, Painter, Romania/USA (1985–): Had her first solo exhibition of paintings at the Whittier Library, in Los Angeles, USA. Nicknamed the "Petite Picasso" for her work, which has sold around the world.

Age 9

Cho Hunhyun, Professional Go Player, South Korea (1953–): Became a professional Go (ancient board game) player. Has since won 150 titles and is considered to be the best Go player in the world.

Age 9

Alma Moodie, Violinist, Australia (1898–1943): Entered the Brussels Conservatory for violin. Became one of the most celebrated female violinists of all time.

Age 10

Ronnie O'Sullivan, Snooker Player, UK (1975–): Made his first century break (a score of a hundred points or more in one go without missing a shot). Later became the youngest-ever snooker player to win a top title when he won the 1993 UK Championship at seventeen years and 358 days old.

Rameshbabu Praggnanandhaa, Chess Player, India (2005–): Became the youngest International Chess Master in history at just ten years, ten months and nineteen days old.

Age 11

Macaulay Culkin, Actor, USA (1980): Starred as Kevin McCallister in the blockbuster film *Home Alone*. One of the most famous child actors in history.

Frank Epperson, Inventor, USA (1894–1983): Invented the popsicle (frozen ice on a stick) when he accidentally left a glass of water with powdered soda and a mixing stick in it outside on his porch during a freezing cold night. He finally patented his invention in 1923.

Age 13

William Wotton, Scholar and Linguist, UK (1666–1727): Graduated from Cambridge University having studied Arabic, French, Spanish, Italian, philosophy, mathematics, geography and history.

Michelle Wie, Golfer, USA (1989–): Won the USGA Women's Amateur Public Links championship, making her the youngest-ever person to win a USGA adult championship.

Age 12

Jet Li, Martial Artist, China (1963–): Won several gold medals in wushu (martial art) at the All China Games, beating adults in their twenties.

Age 14

Tara Lipinski, Figure Skater, USA (1982–): Youngest person ever to win a World Figure Skating title, at fourteen years, nine months and ten days old.

Ian Thorpe, Swimmer, Australia (1982–): Youngest male ever to be selected for the Australian national team, at the age of fourteen years and five months. At the 1998 World Championships in Perth, Australia, he won gold in the 400m freestyle, aged fifteen years and three months, making him the youngest-ever male individual world champion.

Age 15

Chloe Kim, Snowboarder, USA (2000–): Became the first American female to win a gold medal in snowboarding at the Winter Youth Olympic Games, with the highest score in that competition's history at the time.

Age 16

George Nissen, Inventor and Gymnast, USA (1914–2010): Invented his first "bouncing rig" in 1930. The invention became known as the trampoline in 1937.

Age 17

Balamurali Ambati, Ophthalmologist (Eye Doctor) and Researcher, India/USA (1977–): Became the world's youngest doctor at seventeen years, 294 days old when he graduated from the Mount Sinai School of Medicine, USA.

Lorde, Singer-songwriter, New Zealand (1996–): Youngest solo artist (age sixteen) to have a number one on the US *Billboard* Hot 100 since 1987, with her debut single "Royals".

Guptara Twins, Authors, England/Switzerland (1988–): The twins, who were born in England to an Indian father and British mother and now live in Switzerland, published their first novel, *Conspiracy of Calaspia*, which is Book One of their hugely popular *Insanity Saga*.

Barbara Newhall Follett

Novelist – see page 71.

abdicate when a monarch decides to stand down from the throne, giving up his or her duties and power

Academy Award the film industry's biggest award, given for achievement in categories such as Best Actor, Best Actress and Best Picture; also known as an Oscar

activist person who campaigns to bring about political or social change

ambassador important person who represents a government or organization

autism condition that affects a person's communication or behaviour, and how they relate to the world

***Billboard* chart** music industry chart that records sales of singles and albums in the USA

box office how much money a film or play makes based on ticket sales

braille type of written language for blind people, in which letters and numbers are formed by raised bumps that the reader feels with his or her fingertips

CEO chief executive officer, the highest manager in a company or organization

climate change long-term changes to the Earth's climate and weather patterns; thought to be caused by pollution and global warming

code set of rules or instructions made up of words and numbers that tell a computer what to do

Glossary

concentration camp guarded camps where large numbers of persecuted people are held against their will

concerto long piece of classical music written for one or more solo instruments backed up by an orchestra; concertos usually have three sections, or movements

conservation in relation to the environment, the prevention of damage or decay to the planet, its natural resources and its wildlife

contagious type of disease that spreads through contact

debut first time a person does something in public, such as perform or launch an album or book, or play in a tournament or competition

democracy type of government in which the citizens of a country elect their leaders

ecosystem all the living things in an area of nature and the way they affect each other and their environment

entrepreneur someone who sets up his or her own business or multiple businesses

environmentalist person who devotes his or her time to protecting the environment

fax machine device that is used to send and receive documents electronically over a telephone line; a document is scanned, sent and an exact copy printed out upon receipt

Flickr image and video-hosting website

founder person who starts an institution, organization or business

general election type of election during which voters elect people to represent them in government

Grammy Award the music and recording industry's top award, given for achievement in categories such as Album of the Year, Song of the Year and Best New Artist

Grand Slam in tennis, the four most important annual tournaments (Australian Open, French Open, US Open and Wimbledon)

HIV infectious illness that can develop into the disease AIDS; no cure has yet been found but new medicines can help sufferers lead normal lives

hydraulic press mechanical machine used for lifting or compressing large items by applying hydraulic force (liquid pressure)

icon person who is celebrated or idolized by many

indigenous community first inhabitants of a region or country, who were there long before other groups came to settle or occupy those places; also known as native peoples, first peoples and aboriginal peoples

injustice unjust or unfair action or treatment

International Master in chess, one of the highest titles a chess player can attain, awarded by the World Chess Federation

Kickstarter crowdfunding platform that helps writers, artists, filmmakers and designers to get their projects off the ground through donations from the general public

LGBTQ community lesbian, gay, bisexual and transgender community

mentor someone who gives a younger or less experienced person help or advice

monarch king or queen

natural resource naturally occurring thing, such as coal, natural gas, rocks, minerals or fresh water, that is useful to humans

Nobel Prize one of a set of annual awards that recognize extraordinary achievement in various fields, including science, literature and culture

nominee person who is nominated for an award or honour

nonprofit unlike a business, a nonprofit is a charity, organization or programme that uses the money it makes to further its goals

Nuremberg Laws laws introduced in Nazi Germany in 1935 that stripped Jews of their German citizenship and made marriage between Jews and non-Jews illegal

oil rig structure on land or sea that is used to extract oil from deep underground

patent licence that gives an inventor the rights to make and sell their invention, and prevents others from copying them

performance poetry type of poetry written for public performance in front of an audience, rather than to be read in a book

pesticide substance that is used to control or kill pests on crops or animals

PGA Professional Golfers' Association; the women's equivalent is the LPGA

refugee person who leaves his or her country due to war, persecution or a natural disaster

regent person who acts as the monarch of a state on behalf of a king or queen who is ill, absent or too young

shogi ancient two-player strategy board game from Japan, similar to chess

summit meeting between heads of government or other important officials; also refers to the peak of a mountain, or climbing to the top of a mountain

sustainable living in a way that prevents further damage to the environment, wildlife and Earth's natural ecosystems

symphony long piece of classical music written for an orchestra; symphonies usually have four sections, or movements

TED/TEDx Teen Talk short lectures on a huge range of subjects, which can be watched online; TED stands for Technology, Entertainment and Design, while young people give TEDxTeen talks

United Nations global organization formed in 1945 at the end of the Second World War in order to promote peace, human rights, and political and economic cooperation among its member countries

viral if a video or image goes viral, it spreads quickly on the internet and becomes popular or memorable

Find out more

Other books about young heroes:

12 Children Who Changed the World (Change Makers), Kenya McCullum (12-Story, 2016)

Anne Frank (Graphic Lives), Diego Agrimbau (Capstone Press, 2017)

Kieron Williamson: Coming to Light, Keith and Michelle Williamson (Halstar, 2012)

Mark Zuckerberg (Titans of Business), Dennis Fertig (Raintree, 2012)

Mary Queen of Scots (My Royal Story), Kathryn Lasky (Scholastic, 2010)

Michael Phelps (Sports All-Stars), Jon M. Fishman (Lerner Classroom, 2017)

Tom Daley (EDGE: Dream to Win), Roy Apps (Franklin Watts, 2013)

Selected works by the young heroes in this book:

Books

Christopher Paolini, *Eragon* (2003); *Eldest* (2005); *Brisingr* (2008); *Inheritance* (2011)

Jay Hulme, *The Prospect of Wings* (2015) – published under pen name Pixie Hulme

Jordan Romero, *The Boy Who Conquered Everest: The Jordan Romero Story* (2010)

Tavi Gevinson, *Rookie Yearbooks* (Razorbill, 2012–2015)

Dominique Moceanu

Gymnast – see page 51.

Films

Chloë Grace Moretz, *Red Shoes & The Seven Dwarfs* (2018) – Snow White

Daniel Radcliffe, Harry Potter series (2001–2011) – Harry Potter; *Victor Frankenstein* (2015) – Igor

Quvenzhané Wallis, *Beasts of the Southern Wild* (2012) – Hushpuppy; *Annie* (2014) – Annie

Music

Justin Bieber, *My World 2.0* (2010); *Believe* (2012); *Purpose* (2015)

Nobuyuki Tsujii, *My Favourite Chopin* (2010); *Carnegie Hall Debut Live* (2012); *Impressions* (2015)

Taylor Swift, *Taylor Swift* (2006); *Fearless* (2008); *1989* (2014); *Reputation* (2017)

Zara Larsson, *1* (2014); *So Good* (2017)

Websites

STEM

Ann Makosinski
Watch Ann's Google Science Fair video to learn more about her invention, the Hollow Flashlight. Search: **Can I power a flashlight without batteries?**

George Matus
https://tealdrones.com/
See George Matus' super-fast drone in action at his company's website.

Jacob Barnett
Watch Jacob's **"Forget What You Know"** talk at the TEDxTeen website.

Yo-Yo Ma

Cellist – see page 27.

Kelvin Doe
Check out the YouTube documentary that made Kelvin famous.
Search: **15-Yr-Old Kelvin Doe Wows M.I.T.**

Krtin Nithiyanandam
Watch Krtin's Google Science Fair video to learn more about his research into Alzheimer's disease. Search: **Krtin Nithiyanandam – Google Science Fair**

Marita Cheng
https://robogals.org/
Learn more about Marita's work at the Robogals website.

Richard Turere
Watch Richard's TED Talk to learn more about his incredible invention "Lion Lights". Search: **Peace with Lions**

Environment

Birke Baehr
Watch Birke's TEDxTeen Talk about sustainable agriculture. Search: **What's Wrong With Our Food System**

Boyan Slat
Watch Boyan's Slat's TEDxTalk to learn how his Ocean Clean-Up system works. Search: **Boyan Slat at TEDxDelft**

Kehkashan Basu
Check out Kehkashan's inspirational story in this video. Search: **Lifestory Kehkashan Basu**

Maritza Morales Casanova
www.hunab.info/en/
Learn all about Maritza's environmental organization HUNAB.

Misimi Isimi
Learn more about how Misimi is making big changes to the environment. Search: **Meet Misimi Isimi**

Olivia Bouler
www.oliviabouler.net/
Check out Olivia's stunning paintings at her website.

Ta'Kaiya Blaney
www.takaiyablaney.com/
Visit Ta'Kaiya's website to learn more about her environmental work and watch her performances and speeches.

Tom Youngman
Watch Tom's TEDx Talk about his work with Green Vision. Search: **Tom Youngman – Green Vision**

Business

Fraser Doherty
www.fraserdoherty.com/
Learn more about Fraser and SuperJam at his website.

Lily Born
www.imagiroo.com/
See Lily's Kangaroo Cup in action.

Mabel Suglo
Watch an inspirational interview with Mabel, the creator of Eco-Shoes. Search **Eco-Shoes in Ghana**

Mateusz Mach
http://fiveapp.mobi/
Learn more about Mateusz and Five App – the world's first messenger app for deaf people – at this website.

Mikaila Ulmer
https://meandthebees.com/
Learn more about Mikaila's Me & the Bees Lemonade at the company's website.

Tavi Gevinson
www.rookiemag.com/
Visit Rookie magazine's website for all the latest articles and features.

Arts and Literature

Misty Copeland
http://mistycopeland.com/
Learn more about Misty's story at
her website.

Hamzah Marbella
Watch a short documentary about
Hamzah and his amazing paintings.
Search: **Promil Pre-School**
Hamzah Marbella

Politics and Activism

Dylan Mahalingam
www.un.org/millenniumgoals
Learn more about the Millennium
Development Goals at the UN website.
Watch Dylan's"**The Ripple Effect**" talk
at the TEDxTeen website.

Jeremy Heimans
Watch Jeremy's "**Aim Higher Than the**
President" talk at the TEDxTeen website.

Nkosi Johnson
http://nkosishaven.org/
Discover more about the work of Nkosi's
Haven at this website.

Disclaimer: We are not responsible for
the content of the resources included
here, some of which are intended for
an older audience.

The information in this book is up to date
at the time of publication. However, young
heroes and their exciting achievements
are being recognized all the time.
Who knows – maybe you'll beat some of
the records in this book!